Second in Granada's ... e brutal aftermath of a

Wasteworld 2

RESURRECTION

By the same author

Aftermath

JAMES BARTON

Resurrection

GRANADA
London Toronto Sydney New York

Published by Granada Publishing Limited in 1983

ISBN 0 583 13702 4

A Granada Paperback Original

Granada Publishing Limited
Frogmore, St Albans, Herts AL2 2NF
and
36 Golden Square, London W1R 4AH
515 Madison Avenue, New York, NY 10022, USA
117 York Street, Sydney, NSW 2000, Australia
60 International Blvd, Rexdale, Ontario, R9W 6J2, Canada
61 Beach Road, Auckland, New Zealand

Printed and bound in Great Britain by
Cox and Wyman Ltd, Reading
Set in Plantin

For magic . . . for Elvira.

Prologue

It happened gradually, and few foresaw the exact shape of the end.

Like a spreading cancer, the bush wars escalated. There was the Afghan Invasion, but the Western world tended to ignore that. El Salvador was closer to home – America chose to intervene; and intervention bred resentment: the cancer grew larger and stronger. Nicaragua; Guatemala; Honduras: the fighting spread, sucking America inexorably deeper into the chaos. On the other side of the world oil shortage ran hand-in-hand with oil glut. The super powers vied for supremacy, mouthing platitudes as they prepared for war. The Invasion of Cuba brought them to the brink; the Libyan Expedition tipped them over.

The missiles rose. And fell.

Already reeling in the confusion of economic collapse, the West went down into chaos. The conflict was short in its final analysis, and when it was over there was no one left to fight: the world slipped back into barbarism.

A few did see the end. Matthew Chance was one.

He had served his country – as a pilot in the Marine Air Corps – and felt that service turn sour. He had seen the impending holocaust and determined to survive it. He had trained himself to survive, and that harsh discipline had lost him his family. His wife and children had left him, and in the bitter aftermath of divorce he had sought oblivion in the lonely, untouched parts of the world.

He was flying supplies to the isolated islands strung through the southern Indian Ocean when the final conflict erupted, and he had survived it alone.

When it ended, he was still alone. But now he had a purpose: to find his wife and two children again. To know that they were alive – or dead. He determined to return home to the United States and attempt the impossible quest.

But the America he had known no longer existed. In its place was a melting pot of mutations and tribalism, of barbarity and ambition. Chaos reigned. Death stalked alongside deformity. Civilization had collapsed and there was nothing in its place.

America was a wasteworld.

But Matthew Chance had a mission now.

And Chance was a survivor.

Chapter One

Chance halted the Daihatsu and stared at the way ahead. The Interstate was blocked solid with dead automobiles, the bodies inside old enough that even the hot east Texas sun failed to pull any smell off them. Mostly they were bones: in the aftermath of the panic, nature's scavengers had enjoyed a rich feasting. He looked up at the sky. It was hot and bright and blue, striated over to the north with the black wind lines of a high-level storm, but clear around and ahead. It was empty of scavengers now – even the buzzards had fallen victim to the after-effects of the war – and he could see no sign of danger.

He turned the ignition keys in the lock of the four wheel drive overlander and slid them into his pocket before climbing out of the vehicle. He left the M18 Assault Rifle on the passenger-side seat, settling his right hand around the grips of the .44 calibre Smith & Wesson Magnum holstered on his right hip as he moved towards the nearest car.

There were two skeletons occupying the front seats and three small sets of bones curled in the back. Chance did his best not to see them as he checked the petrol gauge. There were worse sights behind him – probably ahead, too – and this family looked to have died easily. There was a .38 calibre Colt Special in the bones of the driver's hands and neat, round holes through the foreheads of all the passengers.

The skeleton in the drive seat was slumped back with most of the skull blown up through the roof. Chance guessed that Interstate 10 had become too hard a road.

Then he cursed as he saw the fuel needle lodge on empty, and walked on to the next auto.

There were two litres of fuel in the tank, so he dropped his hose in and began to work the hand pump, sucking the precious fluid up into the five litre can he was carrying. When the pump cut off on the dry mark he stopped cranking the handle and dragged the hose clear of the auto's tank. He moved on to the next, ignoring the blank, dead bone faces staring at him through the windshield.

It had been like this all the way from New Orleans. When the exodus had begun was impossible to guess, but the roads were jammed with stalled and broken vehicles, their seats occupied by long-dead bodies, or the doors open and the skeletal corpses sprawled over the edges of the highways. It was as though the car-borne nation had sought refuge in its automobiles. And died in them: Chance was glad of the off-trail vehicle the Cajuns had given him: the Daihatsu allowed him to skirt around the insuperable road blocks.

And he was well-equipped. The Daihatsu carried four spare tyres in back, and the tank held enough fuel to give him a range of close on one thousand miles. The M18 was backed by twelve sticks of ammo, and he had two boxes of shells for the Magnum. There were two three gallon tanks of clean water belted to the walls and he was carrying enough tinned food to last him a month or more. The Cajuns had thrown in a comprehensive tool kit that allowed him to handle most running repairs, and – perhaps most useful of all – they had given him a geiger counter.

So far the readings hadn't shown too bad. The strontium count was up, but not over bearable limits. And mostly, it was possible to tell where the big bombs had hit from the craters and the surrounding devastation.

The neutrons were the difficult ones, but by now he was pretty adept at picking out the effects: mostly it meant everything looked normal except for the bodies. They tended to be pools of congealed jelly. He was getting good at spotting them at long range.

The radiation pits were easy to see. There was a glow to them, and the geiger counter started jumping all over the scale. Also, there wasn't anything around them: nothing seemed to live inside the mile-plus radius.

So his journey had been one of deviations. Out of Louisiana on Interstate 10, then across country when the road got blocked up, alternating the off-road travel with patches of secondary blacktops that were mostly clear of stalled vehicles. Now, on the edge of Texas, he needed fuel.

And a human face to talk to.

He filled the gasoline can and took it back to the Daihatsu, emptying it into the depleted tank. The storm to the north was moving closer, great dark lines of worried cloud running across the sky in menacing bands. He could see fork lightning flicker snake-tongued between the striations, and where the lower edge of the clouds touched the horizon, the air was pure black.

He thought about topping the gasoline can again, then decided against it: the way the storm was closing it looked safer to find a hollow.

He climbed back into the Daihatsu and switched on the ignition. The big, eight-cylinder motor churned into life and he switched to four-wheel drive as he spun the wheel to go off the road. The reinforced fender caught the tail of the Chevrolet in front, and he saw the two skeletons in the front seats jerk and fall apart as the car was snapped round. He ignored them, concentrating on taking the Daihatsu down the bank that lined IS10 and into the trench below.

The trench was sanded and as he applied pressure to the accelerator long plumes of dust rose from the rear wheels. They lifted up to where the edge of the trench met the rim of the highway, then the growing wind took them and swirled them around in a great spill of floating sand. The needle of the geiger counter rose higher across the scale as the storm approached. Chance fastened his hands on the Daihatsu's steering wheel and shoved his foot hard against the gas pedal.

The trench ran parallel to the Interstate for almost a mile. It was littered with vehicles that had gone off the road as their drivers died, or been pushed off by the sheer weight of the exodus following behind them. Chance steered round them, skidding the Daihatsu up the banks with all the power of the multiple drive facility and a disregard of fuel consumption. Out here the land was flat – East Texas plains – and the storm was coming in fast and furious: he wanted cover before it hit.

He found it a mile and a half ahead. There was a bridge where a feed road bled into the Interstate, a concrete and metal structure that formed a kind of bunker over the trench. The top side was lined with wrecked automobiles, but the hollow beneath was empty, and he halted the Daihatsu there, glancing at the readout dial of the geiger counter.

The radiation count was getting higher still as the storm got closer and he guessed it was one of the big blows sweeping down from the Rockies, scooping up radioactive waste along its path and spilling the lethal dust over the land ahead. He checked the plastic seals covering the truck's windows and air vents, then settled down to wait for the storm to hit.

It came faster than he expected. The light suddenly faded as the sky got black. Either side of the bridge dust roiled in heavy clouds through which lightning flickered in weird patterns. A coating of yellow-grey plastered the windows of the Daihatsu, and Chance felt the vehicle shake as the first onslaught of the wind funnelled under the bridge. There was a clap of thunder that reverberated through the truck's metal and a car was torn clear of the roadway above. Dimly through the mess covering the windshield he saw that it was a Ford. It landed on its nose, bones rattling inside, then pivoted slowly over to crash down onto the roof. For an instant, Chance saw a bleached-bone skull grinning at him, then the swirling dustcloud hid the automobile. He heard others fall, the clatter of rending metal faint beneath the howling of the storm, and he fastened his hands tight on the steering wheel as the Daihatsu trembled, shaken by the wind.

Vivid flashes of light lit the darkness, and Chance used them to read the geiger counter.

The radiation count was still within bearable limits, though if the storm persisted the overall absorption level could become dangerously high. He hoped it would blow away as fast as it had come. That was usually the way. At least, it had been since his departure from New Orleans.

He had encountered three storms since the Cajuns had provided him with the Daihatsu, but each one had struck where there had been buildings to shelter him from the worst effects. In Baton Rouge he had simply turned into an underground parking lot to wait out the blow; in Lafayette there had been a store he had entered by the simple expedient of driving in through the plate glass windows; and in Goosport he had holed up in an empty church. The Cajuns had warned about the storms. They started way up north, beyond the Canadian border, and blew down clear across the United States. The absence of large heat masses – no longer present with the cities empty and industrial centres dead – meant there was nothing to stop them: they simply blew, gathering momentum all the way down. Gathering, too, radioactive particles from the ruptured atomic plants and wasted missile centres. Effectively, they subjected the southern parts of the country to a constant bombardment of radiation that served to keep the mutation level high. The Cajuns had warned him of that, too: he could expect monsters along the way.

He had seen some. In Baton Rouge he had driven the Daihatsu out of the parking lot over a carpet of outsize rats with teeth that had left gouge marks on the fenders. In Jennings he had shot three dogs with distorted limbs and sabre fangs. One had sported six legs.

Out here on the Texas flat his journey had been mostly uninterrupted: there simply wasn't enough life left to support predators. Except for the insects. He had seen ants the size of his hand, gila monsters big as a man. Twice he had driven through spider silk that draped across the road like heavy-duty netting, the spinners scuttling down to investigate the destruction like creatures from a nightmare. He had driven on each time: he felt an instinctive loathing of spiders, preferring to ignore them rather than investigate their size.

The memory depressed him and he climbed back between the Daihatsu's forward seats to the tail area. There was a mattress there, set between the spare parts and the crated provisions. He checked the level in his water tank and dribbled out a half-cup of the liquid. The air inside the truck was hot and dry, and he felt he could taste the dust outside in his mouth. He drank the water, then reached for one of the bottles racked alongside.

The Jack Daniels sat easy on his tongue. And felt better as it hit his belly. He grunted his appreciation and set the tin cup down on the trembling floor. He thought about switching on the interior lights, then decided against running down the batteries and settled instead for the darkness and the Tennessee sipping whisky.

He took it slow, eking out the cup as the shaking got less and the light got brighter. After a while he sat up, and saw the needle on the geiger counter dropping back close to normal. The bulk of the storm seemed to have blown away to the south and the buffeting of the wind was distinctly eased. He climbed back into the drive seat and flipped the wiper switch. The twin blades skidded over the automatic application of water, the detergent he had mixed in forming a soapy scud on the glass. Clear patches began to appear through the layered dust and he flicked the headlamps on, the beams lancing through grey-yellow mist still filling the air.

He saw the Ford blocking half the way ahead, beyond it a Dodge pick-up. There was a Nissan and a Chevrolet farther down, all of them showing a litter of bones where the dead occupants had tumbled in disarray over the windows and roofs.

He waited until the mist cleared, then started the Daihatsu and shoved the stick into *Forward*. The tyres spun for an instant on loose sand, then the vehicle gained traction and lurched towards the far end of the bridge tunnel. The light was clear now, the sky again blue with the sun shining out of the west into his face.

He reached into the storage compartment for sunglasses.

And as he set them on his face, something landed on the hood of the vehicle.

His first thought was that another automobile had dislodged from the bridge, and he braced himself against the danger of shattering perspex.

Then nightmare took over as he stared into a multiplicity of eyes and *heard* the mandibles scrape against the windshield. He saw eight hairy legs gain impossible hold on the Daihatsu's hood, the bristles coated with grey-yellow dust that almost hid the original colouring. It was reddish-brown, banded with black: the colouring of a red-knee tarantula.

But this tarantula was the size of a man. The head staring in at him was as big as his own, the mandibles clacking against the Daihatsu's windshield as thick as his fore-arms. The thorax was equal to his own chest, and the bulbous abdomen fatter than his entire body. The legs spread six feet out over the hood, gripping the metal so that his view ahead was blocked. He could see the stinger protruding from the tail hooking down over the radiator.

For a moment, panic gripped him.

The black multiple eyes stared at him with obscene indifference.

He felt the shock run through the truck before he heard the dinning of metal on metal as he hit the Ford and the Daihatsu slewed sideways.

Instinct governed his actions. He slammed into four-wheel drive and put his foot hard against the gas pedal. There was a grinding sound and he felt the over-turned Ford give way. Abruptly he slammed the gear shift into reverse and took the truck back, swinging the wheel to the left as he shifted back into forwards drive. The spider swayed on the hood, then regained its balance as Chance steered around the Ford and went up the side of the trench.

It stayed clinging as he came down again and he realized he could not dislodge it.

The mandibles went on scraping at the windshield, and he saw venom drip in thick globules over the wind-scoured paintwork.

The gigantic arachnid was settled heavily over the hood. Its legs were fastened either side, securing purchase as the eyes glared in at the driver and the awful fangs sought to cut through the perspex.

Fighting revulsion, Chance brought the Daihatsu back down into the trench. He felt the impact as he hit a second blown-over automobile and simply drove the truck forwards, grinding his way past the Dodge.

Then he was in the clear.

Except he couldn't see.

The spider was moving forwards, the two front legs wavering over the roof as it sought entry to the prey inside. The bulk of its massive body covered the windshield so that all Chance could see was the loathsome weight of the abdomen and the bristle-like hairs.

He slammed the shift into neutral and snapped the handbrake on. The Daihatsu skidded to a halt that failed to dislodge the tarantula. Chance snatched the M18 off the passenger seat and thumbed the safety catch to the *off* position, setting the fire mode to *auto*.

He switched off the ignition and took a deep breath, staring at the door catch.

Then he settled his right hand around the assault rifle's pistol grip and reached out with his left to open the door.

As it swung back he hurled himself to the side, going out and through in a rolling dive that landed him on his left shoulder. He felt the spider's bristles scrape his face as a leg touched him, and nausea rose in his belly and throat.

He came over on his back with the M18 lifting to angle on the massive head, exigency fighting fear as the mandibles swung in his direction.

Tarantulas were bird eaters.

They could jump.

He couldn't afford to risk the truck.

He felt sand under his back and drove his legs hard down, slamming both feet against the wall of the trench as he pushed himself back and up.

He saw the eyes watch him.

Saw the legs tense, bunching for a spring.

He rolled again, shifting sideways to go across and down the trench.

Shadow blocked the light.

Sand dusted his face as the spider landed.

He rolled on and down, coming up on his knees with the M18 stuck out in front.

The spider hit the sloping wall and spun in its own length, using all its eight legs to turn.

Chance held the trigger down, yelling as flame burst from the muzzle.

Ejected shells spun bright in the sunlight.

There was the smell of scorching hair.

Chance saw the mandibles open to sink into his chest. Then saw them snap tight as the 5.56 mm slugs burst the head apart. Ichor spurted from the tarantula's head. Chance threw himself back as the legs went on running, driving the mutated thing forwards. One struck his ankle as the spider went past him and he crashed back against the Daihatsu with the M18 still blasting bullets into the hairy body.

He landed against the hood and swung round with the assault rifle aimed across the top of the metal. The spider charged halfway up the far slope, then slid back as it turned. Chance squeezed the trigger again. And saw two legs fold. Then a third. The spider slumped to the side. Chance loosed off another burst and blew a fourth leg away. The spider folded, support gone from one side of its body. The remaining legs went on scrabbling at the sand, but the forwards momentum was gone now and it began to twist in a circle. Chance fought his revulsion, triggering the M18 in short, tight bursts.

Ichor exploded from the fat body and the tarantula seemed to sigh as it slumped flat against the sand.

Chance felt the M18 click empty and dropped it on the Daihatsu's hood. He drew the Magnum, levelling the big pistol at what was left of the arachnid's head.

The mandibles clicked together one last time as the man fired. The .44 calibre slug went in through the front of the head and emerged from the abdomen on a great sticky spray of stinking fluid. The spider went flat on the sand. For a little while it twitched, then it was still. Chance reloaded the Magnum and reached inside the Daihatsu for a fresh clip for the M18.

Then he doubled over and vomited up his last meal.

Chapter Two

He stared at his face in the wing-mirror. It looked tired, seamed with lines under the tan and the coating of dust, the blue eyes edged with shadow, the stubble covering his cheeks matching the premature iron-grey of his close-cropped hair. His chin and the front of his shirt were smeared with vomit.

He went around to the tail of the Daihatsu and swung the rear door open, reaching inside for water. Using it sparingly, he cleaned his face. Then he took off his shirt and threw it away across the sand. He fetched a fresh denim shirt from inside the truck and buttoned it over his lean chest. After that he swilled water around his mouth and then closed the rear door.

It was closer towards night now, and the sun was lancing long shafts of red-gold light down the trench. They glittered where they struck the hairs bristling from the giant tarantula's body, and Chance saw that a column of outsize ants was busy about the corpse. Trying not to see it, he climbed back inside the Daihatsu and drove off in the direction of the setting sun.

He kept going until the light faded and a thin, pale moon came up over the flatlands. By then he was clear of the trench and moving across open country that looked like the setting for a Western movie: all sand and saguarro. The big cacti seemed untouched by the holocaust; indeed, it seemed as though the desert plant life had thrived. Mesquite grew in thick clumps and cholla and chaparral grew in profusion between the bushes and the giant cactus plants.

Chance halted the truck where a patch of clear sand showed and made his customary preparations.

Using a hand torch to supplement the waning light he circled the open area, checking for breaks in the undergrowth. He blocked each one with Mesquite and chaparral, dousing the piled brush with gasoline. Then he built a big fire at the centre of the circle and set water to boiling for coffee as he selected cans from the stores inside the Daihatsu. He kept the M18 close beside him as he squatted down to eat, using the A. G. Russell fighting knife to puncture the cans.

He ate sparingly, concentrating on useful protein and fibre: canned beef and beans. It was boring food, but it gave him the sustenance he needed, and the fibrous quality of the beans helped fight off the possibility of radiation-induced cancer.

When he was finished he tossed the empty cans into the fire and climbed inside the Daihatsu. He snapped the doorlocks into place and double-checked the plastic seals on the windows and air-vents. The atmosphere inside the truck was warm, but he felt loath to turn on the air-conditioning unit for fear of running down the battery. He settled for sleeping hot and stretched out on the mattress with the M18 beside him.

Sometime during the night he got woken by a sound from outside. He was unaware of its origin, knowing only that he was awake with the short hairs on the back of his neck standing up. The M18 was in his hands and even before he became conscious of that fact his thumb had snapped the safety catch off.

He eased up on his knees, peering into the semi-darkness.

The moon was still shedding light and the fire was still glowing. But neither spread sufficient illumination that he could clearly see beyond a few feet.

Working fast, he snapped the magazine out of the M18 and replaced it with one loaded on tracer. Then he eased across the tanks stacked in the rear of the vehicle and slid a side window open. He angled the assault rifle out through the window and triggered three shots into the nearest pile of gasoline-soaked brushwood.

The phosphorous bullets traced white lines through the night. Hit the inflammable barriers. And flame exploded into the sky. Chance fired again, traversing the rifle over the other bonfires. Three of the entrances to the site erupted in raw flame. Chance snapped the tailgate open and went out with the M18 spraying phosphorous bullets in a circle around the Daihatsu.

The night volcanoed into fire.

Flame exploded from the gas soaked wood.

Chance heard an angry hissing, and from two sides of the clearing saw gila monsters retreat from the flames.

They were big: three or four feet high at the shoulder, with teeth like blades and massive tails that lashed the undergrowth in fury. He fired at one and saw the head explode in a ball of incandescent bone and blood. He traversed the rifle, dancing lines of white fire down the sides of three more monsters.

Then one came through the barrier of flame, smashing the bonfire apart so that the burning brushwood added to the effects of the phosphorous shells and the entire clearing was suddenly ringed with leaping flame.

Chance emptied the magazine into the creature.

But it still kept on coming.

He could see the mottled black and red flanks and the flat, ugly head, the jaws open wide. He dropped the empty rifle and snatched the Magnum clear of the holster.

The giant gila ran forwards faster than anything that big and ugly had a right to.

Chance fired once.

Twice.

Saw bone and brain explode out through the skull where his bullets went in between the open jaws.

Then he ducked to the side as the lizard charged past him, teeth clacking on empty air. He fired twice into its side. And saw the thing twist round to snap sabre teeth against the rib wounds.

He fired twice more, bracing the heavy pistol in both hands to plant the shells directly through the gila monster's skull. The impact of the .44 calibre slugs shattered the bone, taking most of the lizard's head away in a sticky spray of hide and bone and brain matter.

It charged into a bonfire and began to stink as it broiled. It fell down on its side, rolling over the flames so that they spread wider still as the sun-dried chaparral took fire and began to fill the night with flame.

Chance reloaded the Magnum and the M18. All around him the flat was getting filled with fire. There was a circle around his camp and it was spreading wider as he watched, dancing over the prairie country like some lit firework.

Abruptly he realized an alternative danger to the gila monsters and went back to the Daihatsu. He climbed inside and fastened the doors. Then he put the truck in gear and went out through the ring of fire.

Flame burst from his path and for an instant he saw a heavy lizard head snap teeth towards him.

Then the head was smashed back and away by the reinforced fenders of the truck and Chance felt the wheels bounce over something that gave soggily.

He snapped the headlamps on and drove westwards. Behind him the night was filled with flame, and his mirror showed the contorted images of lizards roasting as they ran from the fire.

He kept on driving.

Continued until the sun broke up the mist of the false dawn.

Then he halted.

He was at the bottom of a dry riverbed. It ran east to west, and he guessed it might have once been a fork of the Brazos.

The sun was hot and strong in the sky. A real Texas sun. He climbed back into the drive seat and took the Daihatsu up the slope.

And as he topped the ridge he saw them.

At first he thought they must be line poles. Then he thought they looked too closely spaced for telegraph wires. And somehow too bulky around the tops. Curious, he halted the Daihatsu and lifted the Nikon 7 x 50 binoculars from the plastic case taped to the passenger seat.

Climbing from the truck he felt an ugly suspicion form in his mind. And as he lifted the binoculars to his eyes and adjusted the individual focusing, he saw the suspicion come true.

The poles ran the length of the facing ridge, lining the horizon from north to south like a fence. They were, he judged, about fifteen feet high, each one straddled with a six-foot cross-member.

And every one had a body pinned to the cross-piece.

Chance brought his focusing in tight.

And found himself staring at the dessicated face of the corpse hanging from the cross. It was a face made old by death. The original age was impossible to guess, because the features had collapsed under the onslaught of time and sun, the skin drawing tight and parchment yellow over bones that stuck out in skeletal determination against the withering. Black eye sockets stared into the binoculars, beneath them a grinning mouth stretched wide in the ecstatic agony of death.

Chance traversed the line. First to the north, then to the south.

Each crucifix told the same story; some older, some more recent. He saw bare bones and mummified bodies; some still wore fragments of ragged hair. Three were recent additions to the ghastly line, flesh still in place and the dark brown rivulets of blood showing where the nails had gone in.

Chance had seen bodies before. Death was no stranger, not after the fighting in El Salvador and Guatemala; not after the Libyan Expedition. But this felt different: this was the homeland, and America was trying to overcome the effects of the holocaust. Wasn't she?

Chance lowered the binoculars and climbed back into the Daihatsu. Whatever lay ahead he had no choice but to go on. Garth Chambers was somewhere in Texas, and he was the only man likely to know where Stephanie and the two kids might be. Maybe even with him – after all, it had been Garth who engineered the divorce – and Chance wanted to know his family was safe. That was the reason he had quit his safe hideaway on the island in the Indian Ocean and made his way back to the States. In the aftermath of the holocaust, the divorce didn't seem to matter; that Stephanie had left him didn't seem to matter. What he wanted to know was that she was safe; and Davey and Jennifer with her. That was why he had come back.

He put the overlander into gear and drove towards the line of crosses.

Closer up, he could see they were set with military precision, each one about six feet from the next, the bases sunk deep so that they stood upright against the onslaught of the winds. The cross-members were mounted high enough that the bodies were beyond the reach of the remaining predators. And each one carried a small card mounted at the head: *State of Texas. Keep Out.*

Beneath the warning there was a stereotyped signature, underlined with the legend: *President*.

Chance recognized the signature, despite the poor quality of the printing and the effects of weathering. It belonged to Garth Chambers.

Chapter Three

Chance went over the ridge with the sun angling the shadows of the crosses against his face. There was a freeway off to his left that he guessed was the continuation of Interstate 10, but it was blocked with automobiles and as sanded over as the desert all around. Some kind of newly-made roadway went off to the northwest in what might have been the direction of Austin. The surface was crude, but it was empty of vehicles, so he turned the Daihatsu that way and began to cruise at an even thirty.

Off the ridge the land dropped to a broad flat, the roadway intersecting in a clear, straight line that climbed another ridge three – perhaps four – miles off. The terrain was flat and yellow, the roadway cutting through chaparral and cholla. Chance held the truck at a steady speed, conserving fuel and allowing himself time to study the way ahead.

Even so, he missed the line of caltrops spread across the roadway.

They were covered with a thin layer of sand, and painted yellow.

There was a second line fifteen feet beyond.

He heard the front tyres hiss air and felt the wheel slew sideways in his hands. Then the rims hit dirt and the rear tyres blew out as he was still fighting the initial skid. The Daihatsu swung tail-outwards across the road, Chance steering into the skid so that the nose pivoted round as the tyres flayed in shreds off the rims and spun into the dirt at the roadside.

The hood dipped, sand spraying in a blinding wave over

the windshield, then the entire body vibrated as it halted. Chance was hurled forwards, the safety belt digging hard into his chest and stomach. His forehead touched the windshield and he reached with reflex precision to switch off the ignition. The movement continued in an automatic sweep that snapped the seat harness open and lifted the M18 from the passenger seat. It went on as he kicked the drive-side door open and threw himself out, curling as he snapped off the assault rifle's safety catch so that he landed on his left shoulder, rolling to come down on his belly with the M18 thrust out in front.

A voice said, 'Drop it!'

When he didn't, a burst of five slugs fountained sand over his face.

Chance spat dirt from his mouth and crabbed sideways towards the Daihatsu. The burst of fire had come from in front and he was hoping to use the overlander as cover: even with the tyres gone, bandits would be loath to waste a good vehicle.

Then a second burst warned of his mistake. It hit metal just above his head as he got under the cover of the Daihatsu's door. Holes appeared in the truck's side, oil bleeding from ruptured lines. Chance swung the M18 round to cover the fresh attack.

He fired a burst of four at the man dropping behind a dune, then glass exploded above his head as fresh guns blew out the truck's windows and the voice said:

'Last chance! Drop it or die!'

Chance put the M18 on the sand.

'Stand up.'

Reluctantly, he climbed to his feet. At least he wasn't dead, which had to mean his attackers wanted him alive.

Three men rose from the sand. They were dressed in vague uniforms of yellow and green, so that they blended with the landscape. One carried a Colt Commando, the other two M16s. They watched Chance nervously as they came forwards.

The man with the Commando said, 'Take off that goddam belt.'

Chance did like he was ordered. And the man said, 'Whitby, go get that stuff.'

Whitby was tall and thin, with mouse-coloured hair. He looked frightened of coming close to Chance and even more frightened of disobeying the order. He held his M16 tight on Chance's belly as he scooped up the belt holding the Magnum and the A. G. Russell knife and draped it over his thin shoulder. Then he grabbed the M18 by the carrying handle and backed away fast.

'All right,' said the leader. 'Who the hell are you?'

'Matthew Chance,' answered the grey-haired man. 'Who are you?'

'I ask the questions here, boy,' said the man. 'You want to stay alive, you just answer them. Otherwise, you keep your mouth closed.'

Whitby giggled: 'That's tellin' him R. G.'

Chance studied R. G's face. It was tanned and hard, brown eyes watching with the automatic caution of a trained soldier. He was a few inches under Chance's six feet, but his body was lean and solid. And he held the Colt Commando with casual expertise.

He was the one to watch, Chance decided. Whitby was a frightened man following orders, and the third man – who looked like an Apache – seemed uninterested.

'So where the hell you think you was goin'?' asked R. G.

'Texas,' answered Chance, the reply eliciting a snigger from Whitby.

'You see the border?' R. G. asked.

Chance nodded.

'An' you can read?'

Chance nodded again.

'So tell me what them signs say.'

'Keep out,' Chance said.

'You shoulda done just that,' said R. G. 'You shoulda heeded what we put up. Then you mighta lived a while longer.'

Chance saw his eyes narrow and could sense the tightening of his forefinger on the Commando's trigger.

'I wanted to see Garth Chambers,' he said. 'I got business with him.'

Surprise showed on R. G's face and his fingers eased clear of the trigger.

'Business? What kinda business?'

'Personal,' Chance said.

Whitby said, 'Kill him, R. G. Let's get it done.'

R. G. said, 'Shut your goddam mouth, Whitby.' Then, to Chance: 'Talk fast, feller. What business you got with the President?'

'He's my father-in-law,' Chance said. 'My wife's father.'

R. G. frowned. Whitby sniggered. The Indian said nothing, his face not changing expression.

'How come you don't have a pass, then?' R. G. demanded.

'I came up from South America,' said Chance. 'I landed in New Orleans. I'm looking for my wife. And my children – Garth Chambers' grandchildren.'

'I don't believe him,' said Whitby. 'He's makin' it up.'

'No.' R. G. shook his head. 'That's too goddam complicated to make up. We best take him to the old man.'

He glanced at the Indian, who nodded, then said to Chance: 'All right, feller, you bought yourself some time. You better be tellin' the truth, though. Or you'll be hanging around the border like them others.'

He beckoned Chance forwards and jammed the Colt Commando hard into the grey-haired man's belly. The Indian came up and fastened handcuffs on Chance's wrists.

Whitby dumped the M18 and the gunbelt inside the Daihatsu. R. G. said, 'Close it up.' And they moved in a tight group over the sand to where an antiquated Jeep was waiting just below the line of the closest ridge. Whitby climbed into the drive seat, R. G. beside him. The silent Indian snapped a chain through the links of Chance's handcuffs, securing his wrists to the roll-over bar, and they started off.

'You ain't tellin' the pure truth,' said R. G., easing round to glower at Chance, 'you're gonna wish we killed you back there.'

Chance shrugged and asked, 'How'd you know I was coming?'

'Saw your fire.' R. G. grinned. 'Jesus! I could see that miles off.'

'There were gilas,' said Chance.

R. G. laughed and said, 'Them, you expected. Not us, I guess.'

'No,' Chance acknowledged. 'Not you. Who are you, anyway?'

'Texas Militia,' answered R. G. 'Under the command of the President.'

'Who's yore step-daddy,' snickered Whitby. 'If you ain't lyin' to us.'

Chance eased forwards, clamping his hands around the roll-over bar to compensate for the bucking of the Jeep.

'That's the truth,' he said. 'How'd he get to be President?'

'Weren't no one else,' said R. G. 'Not after Dallas took a hit. Houston's too close to the coast an' them Louisiana freakies, an' San Antonio got kinda off-limits when the missile base exploded. Austin was like the only city left, an' Garth was there, so he kinda took charge.'

'Why the crosses?' Chance asked.

And R. G. shrugged and said, 'We gotta keep pure. The President'll explain.'

He turned back to face ahead, staring through the speckled

windshield as Whitby took the Jeep fast over the dirt road. Chance glanced at the Indian, who looked back with expressionless black eyes, then settled down to study the terrain.

The road was empty of vehicles, though from time to time he saw hulks settled by the sides. Most of them sported bullet holes in their sides and windshields, and from that he guessed that the newly-proclaimed State of Texas had no need of vehicles. The fact that the three militia-men had not bothered to check the Daihatsu for fuel suggested that they were either well-stocked with gasoline, or confident enough of the vehicle remaining untouched that they felt it safe to leave where it stood. Whichever explanation was valid, it suggested a degree of confidence in the stability of the state.

Yet the vehicle they were riding was ancient. Efficient, and obviously well-maintained, but still antiquated. And their weapons were inferior to his own. The M16s carried by Whitby and the Indian – even the Colt Commando R. G. held – were old models, long out-dated by the M18. None of them wore any side arms, and their uniforms had the rag-tag appearance of stock pulled from old supplies.

The terrain was flat and dead. Every once in a while a building of some kind showed, but they were always fallen-down and overgrown, devoid of any signs of life other than spider webbing or the hulking shapes of the giant gila monsters. Only the road seemed well-maintained, cutting arrow-straight to the north-west through the chaparral and cholla.

Then, around mid-day, there was a barrier.

Chance was close to dozing in the back of the Jeep, lulled towards sleep by the heat and the monotony of the journey. He woke as the steady jouncing motion slowed and became erratic, opening his eyes as shadow covered his face.

He saw R. G. standing upright in the front of the Jeep, left hand braced against the windshield, the right holding the Colt Commando above his head.

Whitby hit the brakes and the vehicle rolled to a stop between the outlines of a roadhouse and a gas station. There had been other buildings once, but they were gone now, bulldozed into the flat so that only humps of weed-covered rubble showed where they had stood. The two remaining buildings faced one another from either side of the dirt road. They were shored up with sections of timber and aluminium, storm-driven sand piled high against their walls, as though allowed to build there for added protection. Only the frontages were clear. The roadhouse showed blank windows with the memories of old menus not quite scoured from the glass. There was a bulwark of sandbags around the door with the long, ugly muzzle of an M60 machine gun protruding over the bags. Across the way the silent gas pumps were surrounded by similar bags, a second M60 set for cross-fire.

Both machine guns sighted on the Jeep as Whitby braked.

'What the hell you doing here?'

A short, bull-necked man came out from the roadhouse. He had a Colt Python on his hip and Captain's bars on the shoulders of his tunic.

R. G. fumbled a salute and said, 'Picked up an intruder, sir!'

'So?' The bull-necked man looked irritable. 'You got poles out there, don't you? You got nails. Why come here?'

'Says he knows the President.' Whitby sounded almost frightened. 'Says President Chambers is his father-in-law.'

'Do that be a fact?'

The bull-necked man moved around the sandbags to come close to the Jeep. Chance saw that his hair was mostly burned away to a frizzle barely covering the mottled tissue of his scalp. His eyes were small and blue, matching the animosity of his small mouth.

'Yessir!' R. G. climbed down from the Jeep. 'I thought I'd best bring him in.'

'Next time,' said the squat man, 'don't think. Just do what you're ordered.'

'Sir?' R. G. looked confused.

'Crucify him,' said the officer. 'Follow orders.'

'But,' said R. G.

'Yours,' said the captain. 'And if you keep mouthing off, it'll be hanging alongside his. Do it!'

R. G. looked at Whitby. Whitby looked at nothing. The Indian smiled at Chance.

Chance said, 'I was married to Stephanie Chambers. Garth's daughter. I got two kids – David and Jennifer –they're Garth's grandchildren.'

'Big deal,' said the officer.

'Be big if you kill me and Garth finds out,' said Chance. 'Might even mean you join me.'

'Talk to me,' said the captain. 'Make it good.'

Chance shrugged. 'Hell! We can all make mistakes. One of the crosses we got to bear.'

The captain stared at him, then said: 'All right. Unlock him. I'll send him up the line.'

Chapter Four

'You ain't telling the truth, I'll personally hammer the nails in.'

Chance looked straight into the small blue eyes and asked, 'What's your name?'

He put sufficient command into his voice that the militia captain replied automatically: 'Bogdanovich.'

He realized his mistake as he said it, but by then it was too late: Chance had taken the advantage.

'Bogdanovich,' he said softly. 'I'll mention that to Garth. Could go either way.'

Bogdanovich's lips puckered as he bit down on a curse. He stared up at Chance with a mixture of pure hate and fear in his eyes. Then he gestured at R. G. and said, 'Get the hell back to your station. And don't bring me no more wanderers. We don't need them.'

Chance watched the Jeep swing round. R. G. and Whitby looked glad to be gone. The Indian swung round to stare back at the grey-haired man, his face impassive as ever.

'All right, mister.' Bogdanovich made the title sarcastic. 'Let's go.'

Chance stuck his arms out and asked, 'You want to take these off?'

Bogdanovich chuckled and said, 'No. An' don't try nothing.'

'I won't,' Chance smiled back. 'I'd hate to lose the chance of meeting my father-in-law again.'

The reminder hit home, and Bogdanovich spun round, bellowing for someone to bring a car up.

A four-wheel drive Dodge pick-up came out from behind

the rear of the roadhouse. There were extra fuel tanks strapped onto the tail, the feedlines running over the sides of the gate. Two men sat in the cab, the man on the passenger side carrying an M16. Bogdanovich gestured with the Python and Chance climbed into the flatbed. The captain smiled evilly and yelled for someone to fasten the prisoner down.

Two men climbed up beside Chance. One stuck an M16 against his ribs as the other fixed the handcuffs to a stanchion. Bogdanovich said, 'Pleasant ride, feller.'

Chance was stretched out on his left side, arms dragged up by the fixings of the handcuffs so that he was unable to rest flat against the bed of the truck. There were corrugations banging against his ribs as the vehicle started off, and his arms were forced into a painful curve around the bulk of one fuel tank. Each time the Dodge bounced over a hump in the road, he was lifted up, arms jerked painfully as he slid back along the panelling. Before long, the handcuffs produced bloody rings about his wrists as his weight hauled him back against their pull. His legs ached with the effort of pushing himself back to take up what slack he could. And his side bruised from the constant bouncing against the bed.

He concentrated on survival techniques, letting the pain in his wrists and arms and side and legs lend him anger as he recited a *hai-ku* that was accompanied by as many deep breaths as he was able to take: *Survival is in the will.*

Survival is in the will.
Survival is in the will.
And I will!

He was barely conscious when the Dodge stopped and they unlocked the handcuffs.

He opened his eyes as he felt the pain lessen around his wrists and hands take hold of his ankles to drag him down the bed of the truck. He forced them to focus on his situation, still reciting the *hai-ku* in his mind.

There were more of the Texas Militia here. Four of five were pointing guns at him as four more lifted him from the Dodge and began to carry him towards the sound of water. He protested. And someone shoved what he vaguely recognized as an ancient M14 against his belly and told him to keep quiet.

Survival is in the will.

And I will!

He kept quiet and let them carry him over to a swaying plank that hung between sand and blue water.

Let them set him roughly on a bed of sacks as a motor churned and he saw spray lift against the darkening sky. There was a big silver moon that reflected back the droplets of churning water. It lit the man crouched in the rear of the boat, and when Chance twisted his head to stare forwards it was lined with the angular muzzles of the two M60s set either side of the bow.

He turned back, checking the stern: the man squatted there was clutching the control rods of a big 80 horsepower Evinrude. There were two men wearing helmets crouched either side, M16s in their hands.

He looked forwards again, and saw four more men hunkered down on both sides of the boat with more assault rifles clutched ready to use. Ahead of them, he could see the men settled behind the machine guns. *My God!* he thought. *It's like South America all over again.*

He eased up so that he could see over the flank of the boat. There was moonlit water churning back from the prow, and when he twisted his head around again, he could see the wake shining silver under the moon.

Someone said, 'Keep yore fuckin' head down!'

And he dropped instinctively. Then asked: 'Where are we?'

The same voice answered, 'The Colorado. Where the hell you think?'

Chance stretched back, relating geography in his mind.

He had been following Interstate 10, but somehow he must have swung north to skirt around Houston. He must have crossed the Brazos because it hadn't taken R. G. and Bogdanovich that long to get him here. And if he was on the Colorado, then he was moving directly towards Austin. Presumably, the Texas Militia used the rivers rather than the roads because the roads were blocked.

By what?

'How come you don't use autos?' he asked.

A shape rose from between the two machine guns, and in the moonlight Chance saw there were lieutenant's markings on his helmet and ragged uniform.

'You don't know?'

The voice was soft, hushed under the swirl of the Evinrude and the desire for silence.

Chance said, 'No.' Equally softly.

'Bandits,' said the lieutenant. 'Goddam traitors. They hit the roads, so we use the water.'

'Not much water in Texas,' said Chance. 'Must hamper you some.'

'Some,' acknowledged the man. 'But we get by.'

'R. G. had a Jeep,' Chance said. 'Bogdanovich had a Dodge. They got through.'

'Border patrols.' There was cynicism in the lieutenant's voice. 'They play it up big, but it's us got the real problems – the ones inside.'

Chance thought about the guerrillas in Cuba and Guatemala and Nicaragua: and agreed.

'You got airpower?' he asked.

The lieutenant's spittle floated briefly on the wake.

'Christ, man! Garth Chambers would give his right arm for a good combat pilot.'

Chance held his face impassive as he asked, 'He don't have any?'

'A few left,' came the answer. 'And they ain't so hot. The others got killed. Along with their machines.'

'How?' Chance asked.

'How come you're so interested?' came the answer.

'I'm a pilot,' came the reply. 'Marine Combat Force.'

'Jesus!'

It was hushed.

'Light aircraft and helicopters.' Chance picked up the advantage. 'The Libyan War. Cuba. The Police Actions.'

'God!' The lieutenant came down the boat to squat where he could see Chance's face clearly. 'You kidding me?'

'No.'

'And you really are the old man's son-in-law?'

'That's right.'

'Man, if you're telling the truth you're laughing. Listen, I was conscripted for service – you want to tell me who you was with?'

'M.C.F.,' said Chance. 'The Death Eagles.'

'Oh, my God!' said the lieutenant. 'If I bring you home to the old man, I could make captain.'

'So do your best,' said Chance. 'Who were you with?'

'The Screaming Eagles,' said the officer. 'But I never saw service. Until now.'

'Good outfit,' Chance grinned. 'Do your best.'

'Yeah.'

The lieutenant nodded and slid back to the prow.

The boat went on up the river.

Sometime around midnight there was rifle fire from the banks that was answered by the sparkling bursts of the M60s and the brief red flashes of the assault rifles carried by the men on the sides.

The heavy machine guns seemed to clear the way, and after a few minutes the firing died away behind them. The officer came back to check that Chance was safe. And seemed delighted to find his prisoner still alive.

Chance was delighted, too.

Especially as it was beginning to appear that he was a rare commodity.

Even one with an opportunity to stay alive.

Chapter Five

Austin looked clean.

As the boat pushed up the river under the Longhorn Crossing Dam there was no sign of damage to the buildings: only an absence of people. Chance watched the empty buildings go by, waiting for faces to show. None did until they docked against the dam and he was escorted from the boat onto a wharf that was lined with soldiers.

The lieutenant – Chance had learnt his name was Bergstrom – clambered onto the wharf and fidgeted with his uniform.

A major appeared and Bergstrom saluted. Chance saw that both officers and all the men wore the same faded uniforms as R. G. and Whitby and the Indian. But the men lining the wharf carried matched weapons: M17s. And their boots were clean as Marines' on drill parade. He saw Bergstrom point towards him and the major nod, then he was beckoned forwards.

The major was tall, hawk-featured, with tinted glasses on his eyes. Chance noticed that he wore a flak jacket and a Ruger Magnum in .44 calibre belted cross-draw style on his left hip.

They looked at one another, then the major said: 'I hear you claim to be related to the President.'

'I am,' said Chance.

The major looked at him, eyes moving slowly up and down Chance's lean frame.

'If you're lying you'll be godawful sorry.'

'I'm not.' Chance stared back into the reflective surfaces of the sunglasses.

'All right.'

The major nodded, motioning for the lieutenant to take

Chance through the watching squad of armed men. Bergstrom waved Chance on, and four men from the boat fell into step behind them.

Dawn was breaking now, the sky over to the east getting bright. It lit up the outlines of the skyscrapers running back from the wharf towards the centre of the city. Sunlight shafted between the tall buildings in thin streamers of brilliance, emphasizing the emptiness of the streets, sparkling off blank windows and polished doorways. There were no vehicles and no bodies. There weren't even, Chance noticed, any predators: no rats or wild dogs or feral cats. The streets were pristine.

'How come?' he asked Bergstrom. 'New Orleans was crawling with vermin.'

'This ain't New Orleans.' There was a note of pride in the officer's voice. 'This is Austin.'

Chance shrugged. 'Same problems.'

'Not here,' said Bergstrom. 'The President got Texas organized. Civilization starts in Austin.'

'Yeah.'

Chance thought about the crosses marking the border and didn't say anything more.

They marched on down a wide street he didn't recognize and swung left into an avenue with signs that read *President Street*. When he had visited the city before there had been different signs – he felt sure of that as they approached the big building with the stars-and-stripes and the Texas state flag cross-hung over the entrance.

This one had been the Chambers Building, he thought. Now it carried a legend above the entrance that said it was the *Presidential Palace*.

Bergstrom halted at the foot of the steps leading up to the flag-hung portico. Chance looked at the sandbags around the doors and the M60s mounted there.

A man in a blue and yellow uniform with captain's brevets on his shoulders came down the steps and halted three above them. Chance thought he looked like some Ruritanian fantasy. But the Ingram holstered on the fancy beading of his right hip was real enough.

Bergstrom saluted and barked: 'Lieutenant Bergstrom reporting, sir. With a prisoner.'

The captain returned the salute lazily.

'Lieutenant?'

'He claims to be the President's son-in-law.' Bergstrom said it fast. As though trying to justify himself. 'And he says he's a pilot. Light aircraft and helicopters.'

'Bring him up.'

The captain beckoned the squad forwards and Chance went up the steps towards the machine guns. Between them. And into the building.

Inside, the air was cold, the morning not yet warm enough to heat the marbled interior.

There was a double stairway curving round from the groundfloor to a wide balcony. Soldiers with fixed bayonets stood guard at the feet. Between them, and set several yards in front, was a desk manned by an officer with an even more ornate uniform than the captain's. Either side of the desk stood two troopers with M16s.

The captain halted an exact three feet out from the desk and saluted.

The officer behind climbed slowly to his feet and returned the salute.

Bergstrom stood to rigid attention.

'Lieutenant Bergstrom reports an intruder,' said the captain. 'One claims he's related to the President.'

'Send the lieutenant forward,' said the officer. And the captain snapped round neat as a Marine drill sergeant and barked the order.

Chance was too far back to hear the muttered conversation, but seconds later the officer nodded and gestured for him to approach the desk.

A rifle's muzzle prodded him in the small of his back and he stepped forwards.

The officer looked at him, then at Bergstrom. Then he said, 'You better not be lying.' And picked up a telephone set under his desk.

Chance heard only one side of the conversation: 'Sir? Major Bland here. There's a prisoner claims to be the President's son-in-law. Yessir! Matthew Chance. Tall. Grey hair. I'd say, in his thirties. Sir? Of course. Rightaway!'

He set the phone back on its cradle and looked hard as he could at Bergstrom.

'You did well, Lieutenant. I'll mention this in the report.'

Then he looked at Chance and said: 'You! Get up stairs. The President wants to see you now.'

Chance grinned.

Shrugged. And held his hands out towards the officer.

'You want to take these off first?'

Bland glared at him and started to shake his head.

Chance said: 'I can't fly with torn-up wrists.'

Bland nodded reluctantly and motioned for Bergstrom to loose the handcuffs.

'Thanks.'

Chance shook his wrists and moved towards the stairs.

Bland's face went dark with rage, but he fought it down and motioned for the guards to let Chance pass. The tall man ducked his grey head and began to climb up the steps towards the balcony.

At the head a soldier gestured him towards a massive set of double doors. Two more opened them as he approached. He looked into the room, massaging his bloody wrists, and said:

'Hello, Garth.'

Chapter Six

The room was long and high-ceilinged. At the far end massive windows rose from floor to roof, the morning light spilling in through the thick glass to paint the antique veneer of the wood panelling with rich red-gold. Bookshelves lined both sides, the leather-bound spines glowing chestnut and red in the light. The floor was polished pine, paler than the other woods or the leather of the books so that it seemed to lead the eye towards the desk at the far end.

The desk was a gigantic mahogany structure, sitting solid as a battle tank before the windows. A bronze American Eagle stood to one side, three telephones and an intercom unit on the other. To the left, between the desk and the bookshelves, there was an American flag; to the right, there was the flag of Texas. Behind the desk there was a massive, swivel-back chair. Seated in the chair was a balding man with a jowly face and a fleshy mouth. With the light shining into his eyes, Chance couldn't make out the features too clearly. But he could remember them all too well: the eyes would be small and baby-blue, overhung with thick, silver brows; the mouth would be wide and thick; there would be liver spots on the balding pate; more on the powerful hands.

His boots clattered on the pine flooring as he walked forwards and he smelled fresh polish and the faint tang of after-shave. The man in the chair gestured, and the soldiers swung the doors closed.

'Hallo, Matthew,' said Garth Chambers. 'I thought you were dead.'

'No.' Chance shook his head and sat down in the high-back chair facing the desk. 'I'm a survivor.'

'One of the few things I always admired about you,' Chambers acknowledged. 'How?'

'After the divorce?' Chance asked bitterly.

'That and the Trouble.' Chambers set a capital on the last word. 'Tell me.'

'I sold up,' Chance shrugged. 'The airline brought in enough to cover debts and buy me a plane. I worked for the French – a scientific research outfit down in the Indian Ocean. You know the Crozet Archipelago?'

When Chambers shook his head, Chance continued: 'Not many do. I was there when it started. I stayed down there until it was over. Then I came back. I want to find Steph and the kids.'

'How did you get back?' demanded Chambers, ignoring the implicit question in Chance's voice. 'That's a long way.'

'I made South America,' Chance answered. 'Before I ran out of fuel. I worked my way up to Louisiana.'

'How?' Chambers toyed with a pen. 'I hear it's tough down there.'

'No more than anywhere else.' Chance contained his impatience. 'I ran coke. I flew. I made enough to set up a deal.'

'You came out of Louisiana,' said Chambers. 'That's Cajun country. Nigger country. They got mutants there.'

'They helped me.' Chance remembered Alice Adams. 'The Cajuns gave me the Daihatsu your people shot up.'

'They had orders.' Now Chambers shrugged. 'Our borders are closed.'

'Why?' Chance demanded.

Chambers smiled at him. Lazily. Knowingly. It was an expression Chance remembered: and hated.

'We're pure,' said the old man. 'We may be the last pure

folk in this great country. We have to stay that way. That means keeping our borders closed.'

'By killing anyone who crosses them?' Chance asked.

'No one has to,' said Chambers. 'The warnings are clear enough.'

'Yeah.' Chance thought about the crucifixes. 'That was your idea?'

Chambers ducked his heavy head in agreement. 'I am the President. And before you ask why or how – by natural selection.'

'You always were the one to see the main chance,' grunted the grey-haired man. 'So now you run what's left of Texas?'

'Something like that,' Chambers agreed. 'A strong man is needed to get things back in order – I'm that man.'

'Sure.' Chance thought about Amos, back in New Orleans. 'Where's Steph?'

'Not here,' said Chambers. He saw Chance's features tense and added quickly, 'I don't know where she is.'

'The hell you don't!'

Chance lifted from the chair in a single lithe movement that set both his hands around the old man's throat. He saw a liver-spotted hand reach towards the intercom unit and knocked it aside. Chambers struggled for breath. Chance stretched across the desk, trapping Chambers' left hand in his right as he sunk the fingers of his left into the man's windpipe. He enjoyed the way the President's eyes bulged, and the purpling of his visage. Chambers scrabbled at the hand cutting off his air supply, his fleshy lips opening like a fish's as his tongue began to protrude.

Chance eased his grip slightly.

'Where is she?'

'I don't know.' Chambers' voice was hoarse. 'I swear it.'

'Where are the kids?' Chance asked.

'Gone.' The answer was a breathless whisper.

'God damn you,' snarled Chance. 'I'm going to kill you.'

He squeezed Chambers' throat until the old man's eyes rolled up to show white. Then he let go, allowing the heavy body to flop back against the chair as he slid clear of the desk. He was starting to move around it when the old man opened his eyes again. They were lizard-cold, the blue emphasized by the livid shading of his cheeks.

'You shouldn't have done that, Matthew.'

'The hell I shouldn't!' snarled Chance.

The desk was big enough that he was only partway around it when the door burst open and five soldiers led by Major Bland poured into the room. Bland had an Ingram in his hand. The troopers were pointing M16s. All at Chance.

The grey-haired man froze.

The troopers spread out to either side of the room as Bland advanced, positioning themselves so that they could hit Chance without damage to either the Major or the President.

'You're a goddam fool,' husked Chambers, massaging his bruised throat. 'You'll pay for that.'

Chance watched Bland get closer. The man was holding the Ingram in his right hand, his left lifted in a warning gesture. Chance backed away as though frightened.

Bland said, 'Stay still, you bastard!'

And Chance replied: 'You left it too long. You fire that thing now, you'll hit ole Garth.'

Bland saw his mistake: Chance had backed up far enough that he now stood directly between Bland and Chambers. If the officer squeezed off the .45 calibre mini-gun, the spray of slugs would irrevocably hit Chambers. His face went pale under its tan and he opened his mouth to give an order to the watching troopers.

Chance said, 'Ricochets!'

And Chambers gasped: 'Don't fire!'

Bland started to lower the Ingram. And as he did so,

Chance came back around the desk, using its surface as a pivotal base for his arms as he set both hands flat on the polished wood and lifted his feet off the floor.

The double-footed kick took Bland in the stomach. Breath gusted from his suddenly-gaping mouth and he doubled over the pain in his belly. Chance let his momentum carry him on round, swinging off the desk to drive the edge of his left hand down hard against Bland's wrist. The Ingram stuttered bullets into the floor, then Chance was twisting it clear of the major's grip.

The machine pistol dropped to the floor.

Chance stooped to retrieve it as Bland went down on his knees and face. Then, with a final despairing gesture, the major thrust out his hands to send the deadly little gun skidding across the polished wood. Chance cursed and rammed an elbow against his neck. Bland's eyes crossed and closed and his head went down to thud his chin hard against the floor.

Chance went after the Ingram. But by then it was too late.

There were already troopers crossing the polished wood with their rifles lifted. Chance touched the Ingram. Then felt pain as a boot crashed against his wrist and another kicked the machine pistol across the room. A butt smashed between his shoulders and he grunted in pain as he was slammed against the pine. He started to get up, but more rifles landed butt-down against his shoulders and back and legs. He felt the air smashed from his lungs as agony exploded down his spine and ribs. A boot ground against his outstretched hand. More thudded into his sides.

Dimly through the pain he heard Garth Chambers say, 'You made a bad mistake, Matthew. A real bad mistake. Now you have to pay for it.'

Chapter Seven

Chance opened his eyes on a stark white room.

The first thing he saw was the ceiling, which was white. When he turned his head, he saw white walls. A white sheet was drawn over his body, and when he eased to a sitting position, he saw white pillows on a plasticised white bed-frame that was set on a white floor. There were no windows, and when he studied the walls, he could see no sign of a door. The only break in the uniformity of the room – apart from himself – was the white plastic panel in the centre of the ceiling that lit the place.

He swung his feet off the bed, wincing as the movement sent shafts of pain lancing through his body. He looked down at his ribs and saw bruises mottling his skin, then clutched his head in both hands as a wave of nausea hit him.

He felt like throwing up, but there were no facilities in the room: it was bare of anything save the bed. He fought the nausea, utilising the concentration techniques picked up in the Marines and during his survival training. And after a while it went away and he stood up.

His ribs and back were bruised, but there didn't seem to be anything broken. There was a lump the size of an egg on the back of his skull, but if that blow had concussed him, he was over it now. He looked at his arms and saw needle marks: he had received medical attention. He paced out the room: four in both directions. When he reached up, he was able to touch the ceiling with his fingertips. He explored the walls and finally located the door. It was set into the plastic moulding so smoothly it was barely visible, directly opposite the bed, although there was no evidence of a spy-hole.

He guessed there must be a camera in the light fitting, recognizing the disorientation technique, and went back to squat on the bed.

He recited the hai-ku in his mind:

Survival is in the will.

And I will.

He kept it up for what he estimated was half an hour, then tested his body with exercises.

His ribs and back were badly bruised, curtailing the routine of muscle-building press-ups and sit-ups and slowing the balletic movements of the Ap Kai Do work-out. When he was finished, he settled on the floor in the lotus position and concentrated on slowing his heartbeat. He refused pointblank to worry.

With calm forced on his mind, he went back to the bed and stretched out.

After a while, he slept.

When he woke again the room was the same. The texture of the light was unaltered: the only indication that time had passed, the hungry ache in his belly.

There was no sign of food.

He grinned to himself and performed the Ap Kai Do routine again.

Then he slept some more.

When he next woke, he felt a lot more hungry. He went through the full exercise technique and dropped onto the bed more exhausted than he thought he should be.

He slept, finally. But it was a sleep disturbed by dreams of food and Stephanie. He woke angry with himself and hurled into the routine before concentrating on the hai-ku, then sleeping again.

The light in the room remained constant: it was always bright. And the temperature remained exactly the same, around 64 degrees, neither hot or cold. He felt cold, though, because he had received no food. Which was both good and bad: he was conscious of growing weaker, but the absence of nutriments meant that he did not defecate very often. And without facilities, that made the cell a slightly more liveable place.

He was constantly thirsty: while he slept a litre of water was placed inside the cell. He drank it sparingly, using some to clean his body, and it forced him to urinate. He used one corner for that purpose, sacrificing one pillow as a sop to the inevitable spillages of his body.

The cell began to stink. Even though after what he estimated was three days, he ceased excreting, he still urinated, and the combined odours filled the small space with a heady reek. It was a problem: the hunger was something he had trained to live with, but the last few years had accustomed him to a life of relatively fresh air, so the stench of his faeces and the urine affected him more than he allowed to show.

By his estimate, it was five days before the door opened and Garth Chambers appeared.

He was settled on the bed, reciting the hai-ku. He held his face straight and calm as the old man stared at him.

He said, 'Hallo, Garth.'

'Christ!' There was grudging respect in Chambers' voice. 'You know how long it's been? Ten days!'

Chance kept the surprise off his face: survival training: don't let the enemy know you're confused.

'You was hospitalized for three days,' said Chambers. 'You been in here for seven.'

'That a fact?' said Chance.

'Never had anyone lasted longer than three,' said Chambers. 'You ready to talk yet?'

'About what?' Chance got off the bed. 'Where's Steph and the kids?'

Chambers turned out of the doorway and said, 'Dress him. Clean him up. Then bring him to me.'

Showered, shaved, and fed, Chance felt a whole lot better. Not good, but better. They gave him fresh clothes –underpants and socks and a shirt in the same shade of tan, then olive-drab pants and a blouson; black boots and a belt. Then they took him out to meet Garth Chambers again.

The fresh air tasted good.

He sucked it in as he walked out of the building with two soldiers pointing Ingrams at his ribs and saw Chambers standing to one side of what looked like a drill square with his hands clasped behind his back and a thoughtful expression on his face.

The centre of the square was filled with men. Most of them were chained together, ankle to ankle; the others were soldiers with guns in their hands.

'See that?' Chambers turned as Chance approached. 'That's what happens to rebels and dissidents.'

'Unless they're crucified,' said Chance.

Chambers laughed and said, 'Take him out and show him.'

And the soldiers prodded Chance forwards to join the tail of the column shuffling from the square.

They climbed into trucks and drove out through the city to the Bergstrom Airforce Base. The prisoners were unloaded and ushered off in chained lines to clear debris from the runways. They were divided into teams of five, the chains unlocking at those intervals so that they worked in units, no individual able to escape without the support of his fellow prisoners; no five-man unit able to move fast enough to outrun the guns of the guards.

Chance watched them clear runway 1A. Saw them drag debris from the engines of a stalled Boeing 750. Watched them strip down a Bell-Huey.

They worked hard, under the constant watch of the guards. From the height of the sun when he arrived, he estimated it was around eight in the morning. It was sunset before the guards gathered the teams in and loaded them back on the trucks. They had not been given any food or any water during that time.

'Well? What d'you think of our labour system?'

Garth Chambers stood inside the doorway of Chance's cell, two troopers ahead and to either side, both with Ingrams pointed at Chance.

The grey-haired man said: 'It stinks.'

Chambers laughed and said, 'It works.'

'Slave labour?' Chance grunted.

'They had a choice.' Chambers shrugged from behind the protection of the Ingrams. 'To serve one way or another. They chose their way.'

'What's the alternative?' Chance demanded.

'Armed Forces,' said Chambers. 'Of course, you need some skills – like you got.'

Chance sat on the bed and stared at the liver-spotted old man. 'They were all white,' he said. 'I didn't see one negro or a single mutant.'

'You wouldn't.' Chambers' smile remained the same. 'Like I told you – Texas is pure.'

'There were no Mexicans, either,' Chance said.

And Chambers shook his head and went on smiling that benign, malevolent smile.

'We're getting rid of them, too.'

'My God!' Chance straightened his back in surprise. 'You're a goddam fascist. You sound like a Nazi.'

'You ever read *Mein Kampf*?' asked Chambers. Then, when Chance shook his head, added: 'There's a lot to it. A lot of sense.'

Chance's eyes got wider as the shock hit him.

'You really mean that stuff about keeping Texas pure?'

'Got to,' said Chambers. 'Why we keep the borders closed. Hell! You don't do that, you get a whole lot of riff-raff spilling through. You get Cajuns and niggers and mutants coming in from all over. You get Mexes trying to cross from the south. I have to keep the borders closed so we can keep the State pure.'

'You call it pure?' Chance grated.

And Chambers smiled some more as he nodded.

'Sure I do. It's as white as I can make it. And I aim to keep it white. It's the only way.'

'You're crazy,' said Chance.

'Like a fox,' Chambers grinned. 'Come see.'

The two soldiers stepped forwards as he gestured at them and motioned for Chance to stand up. The grey-haired man obeyed, then followed Chambers' beckoning hand out of the cell with the Ingrams pointed at his back.

He went out by a different route this time, down long corridors of antiseptic white that led to a flight of stairs. Chambers went up the stairs in front, then Chance, unpleasantly conscious of the sub-machine guns aimed at his back. At the head of the stairs a guard opened a metal door and they swung into a corridor with opaque windows letting in light. Chance guessed he must have slept the night away, because the light felt like mid-morning.

They reached a guarded door at the far end and Chambers ordered the soldiers to open it.

When they looked at him askance, he said: 'It's all right – he won't try anything. Will you, Matthew?'

Chance shook his head.

Chambers said, 'Bland is still in hospital, by the way. You broke two ribs and most of his fingers.'

'He wasn't very good,' said Chance.

And Chambers nodded in agreement.

'No. You showed that to me. Now let me show you something.'

The doors swung open and they stepped onto a balcony overlooking the first square Chance had seen. As best he could tell, this one was on the rear side of the building. He tried to orientate himself as they marched briskly along the balcony to skirt the side of the complex.

Chambers halted and said, 'Look.'

Chance looked at an area of flattened rubble where the adjacent structures had been bull-dozed across a patch of ground the size of two football pitches. Tarmac had been layed over the rubble and a runway cut a half mile out to the west.

'Tell me what you see,' said Chambers.

Chance looked down at the sunlit blacktop and knew he was being tested.

'I see a Thunderbolt,' he said. 'Close air support vehicle. Single seater. Looks to be the old A-10A. Runs on those two turbofans mounted in front of the tail – there, they don't show on infra-red so much. It looks to be carrying the 30mm tank-buster – the Avenger – and the standard pylonage for external loads. Fragmentation, napalm – whatever. It's got a maximum speed of around 380mph to 460mph, depending on what it's carrying. The pilot sits in an armour-plated bath.

'And you're never gonna let me fly it.'

Chambers husked laughter and said, 'You're damn' right. What else?'

Chance took his eyes off the grey, squat aircraft and said, 'A Grumman Mohawk. Designed as a battlefield surveillance craft, but you've got it rigged to carry weapons. I'd guess a 0.50in gun and drop tanks filled with napalm. Or phosphorous.

'Beyond that,' he pointed past the second aircraft, 'is a Cayuse. One Allison turboshaft flat-rated at 278shp. One of the sweetest choppers ever made. Cruises at around 150mph with a 380 mile range. It's one of the most compact flying machines in history. It can carry troops or it can carry weapons – torpedoes, missiles, or bombs. You name it.

'After that you got a couple of Cobras. And Garth, why the hell are you wanting all this?'

'Checking,' said Chambers. 'Making sure you still remember.'

'Christ!' snapped Chance. 'You think I could forget Salvador? You think Cuba was a picnic?'

'I wondered,' said the old man who had made himself President of Texas. 'Lately, you've been sounding like some bleeding-heart liberal.'

'I got sick of it.' Chance stared at the combat choppers as he spoke. 'I got a bellyfull.'

Abruptly, he spun to face Chambers, ignoring the mini-guns that pointed at him.

'Listen,' he snarled, 'I'll tell you about one mission we flew. Just one! There were others, but I remember this one better than most.

'It was Salvador. We wanted to take out some rebel villages, so M.C.F.I. – my bunch, Garth. You remember the Death Eagles? – we got the job. We had four of those Cobras. Christ! They were fast: 219mph; and guns all over. A Puff, grenade launchers, rockets, three-barrel cannon. Those babies had it. But what we did was load them up with cordite. Drums of the stuff. You know that cordite's got a burning temperature of 2,200° Fahrenheit? That's hot, Garth. That's about as hot as hell must be. Maybe hotter, because it doesn't leave anything behind to suffer.'

He looked away from the baby-blue eyes towards the two Bell 209 Hueycobras sitting squat on the runway, like waiting spiders.

'We cut the filthy stuff down into strips. About twelve inches by two. Like ribbons. Then we loaded the Cobras and flew in over the jungle. Two villages. Two choppers each. I was leading the flight on target A. There were marines in back pouring the cordite ribbons out through the doors.'

His fingers fastened tight on the rim of the balcony, knuckles showing white through the tan. He went on staring at the helicopters.

'It was like fucking snow, Garth! It went drifting down like fucking snow. I swung the chopper round so that it all fell on the village. I saw kids coming out to pick it up.

'Then we dropped flares.'

His hands gripped the balcony tighter. His eyes were hard and cold, not forgiving himself. Denying even the luxury of tears.

'2,200° Fahrenheit, Garth. You know what that does to a body? It was like watching wildfire run over the ground. They burned. Their huts burned. The goddam jungle burned. I took the chopper up to get away from the heat. You could feel it, you see. And I could still see. I could see the kids burning. I could see their mothers burning.'

'It was a mission,' said Chambers. 'You had orders.'

'Sure.' Chance's head ducked briefly, his eyes still blank. 'I had orders. From Command. Sitting safe in Mexico. Combat Command sitting off-shore in a goddam battleship.

'But I was flying the goddam chopper!'

He lifted his head, turning back to face Chambers.

'When you ignite cordite strips, Garth, they burn. You don't know what heat is. They take the flesh off the bones and then melt the bones. We went in afterwards. All we found was burning. There weren't even many bones left. There was just a fucking great hole. All charred. All black.'

One of the guards was looking sick. The other was licking his lips. Chambers was impassive.

'Listen,' he said. 'You just proved you know your aircraft. Now I got two support planes out there and three helicopters. I don't have many men capable of flying them. Bland was one, but you put him in hospital. You're right when you say I won't let you up in that Thunderbolt, because that's a single-seater. But the others all leave room for someone to watch you. And I need good pilots.'

'Sorry.' Chance shook his head. 'I done my share of crucifying people. I'm not your man.'

'You saw the chain-gangs,' said Chambers, still smiling. 'You want that?'

'No,' said Chance. 'I want to find Steph and the kids. I want to know they're all right.'

'Listen,' said Chambers. 'I'll tell you the truth and offer a deal.'

'What?' Chance looked into the baby-blue eyes, not trusting them, but too afraid to reject the opportunity.

'Stephanie went to some crazy religious colony,' said Chambers. 'Somewhere in Utah. Then I heard she moved to California. David and Jennifer were with her until then. After that, I don't know.'

'That doesn't tell me a lot,' argued Chance.

'It's as much as I know,' Chambers countered. 'But I could maybe find out more.'

'In return for what?' Chance asked.

Chambers smiled and said, 'For what you're good at. Killing people.'

Chapter Eight

'All right.'

Chance started the 1,800hp Twin Pac and watched as the 44ft rotors swung into life. The Cobra shuddered, a vibration running through the bodywork like some old memory. Ahead and below him, the gunner clutched the grips of his 30mm cannon; behind, the four troopers clung to their seats and waited for the chopper to lift.

Chance took it up fast, lifting at close on maximum climb rate to 9,000ft. He hovered there for a while, listening to the UAC motors, then swung the helicopter around the sky over Austin as he tested its capabilities.

'Oh, God!' Lieutenant Bergstrom spoke from behind him in the cabin. 'You have to do this?'

Chance grinned and pushed the throttle forward, sending the Cobra into a 200mph sweep to the west.

Bergstrom settled pale-faced into his chair. The soldiers clutched at their battle harness and tried to ignore the belly-emptying rush of acceleration.

Chance crossed the city in seconds, moving out along the line of Highway 290. They crossed Oak Hill and Dripping Springs, then passed over Johnson City and Fredericksburg to catch the line of Interstate 10 beneath them. The highway was lined with vehicles, but nowhere was there any sign of movement.

He took the chopper down low, watching as dust billowed about the automobiles. Still nothing moved. Bergstrom consulted a map and reached forward to tap Chance's shoulder.

'There was movement reported in this area.' He shouted

over the thunder of the rotors, indicating the grid reference. 'Let's check it out.'

Chance nodded and swung the Cobra off in a south-westerly direction. Below them the land lay flat and arid, thick with cactus, as though the undergrowth was reclaiming the country. Chance held the chopper at a steady 150mph, wondering at the total absence of animal life.

'Not much left,' Bergstrom yelled when Chance questioned him. 'There are some wild horses left – cattle, too – but mostly they got eaten. The wild dogs stay mostly in the cities, but we're getting rid of them. We shot out most of the mutants, so generally you only see the gilas and the spiders around the borders.'

'You got it organized,' grunted Chance.

'Yeah!' Bergstrom nodded enthusiastically. 'Thanks to President Chambers – he really got things together.'

'Drastically,' Chance muttered, thinking of the crosses and the chain-gangs.

'No other way,' said Bergstrom, earnestly. 'These are hard times, and hard times call for hard measures. Hell! We're protecting civilization. So far as we know, we're the only organized state left.'

'You got no outside contact?' Chance was surprised. 'Don't you hear anything by radio?'

'No.' Bergstrom shook his head. 'With limited power supplies we don't get too much range. Oklahoma's silent – they got hit badly up there – and most of New Mexico's wasteland. There's interference from the radiation, too; and the freak storms. We're pretty much on our own.'

Which, Chance thought, is just how Garth would like it. In place of his business conglomerates he's got a state to play with.

'There!' Bergstrom interrupted his thinking. 'That has to be it.'

Chance eased their speed down as the helicopter breasted

a low ridge. Over the rim, the terrain dropped away in a sweeping bank that curved around to the north, cradling the grazing land that spread along the bottom. A stream cut through the grass, coming out of the slope to the north. Close to where the stream emerged there was a building.

Chance put the Cobra into the hover mode, studying the building.

It looked as much block-house as ranch-house. Built partially into the slope itself, it extended a flat roof out over the grass, solar panels gleaming bright in the morning sun. The roof shaded an upper balcony that would afford a clear view over the entire bowl. The walls were white, and Chance guessed that was anti-radiation coating over solid concrete. Windows showed dark on the two walls he could see, and the entire structure was surrounded by a high, barbed wire fence.

He eased the column forwards, taking the helicopter gently around the building. On the far side there were two tall windmills adjacent to a flat, slab-like structure that he guessed was a generating station.

'Set us down,' Bergstrom ordered.

Chance studied the distance between the barbed wire and the house: it was too close.

'It's got to be outside the fence,' he warned.

'Just do it!' Bergstrom was checking the safety on his M17.

Chance shrugged and dropped the chopper smoothly onto the grass. Cattle bellowed and ran from the clatter of the rotors. Bergstrom and his men jumped from the machine and ran for the fence.

There was a big gate set in facing the front of the building. It had a heavy-duty built-in lock. Bergstrom cursed as he tried – and failed – to open the gate.

Chance climbed leisurely from the pilot's chair, leaving the gunner alone. He stayed close to the Cobra: he was unarmed and it looked as though Bergstrom was getting ready to attack. He had his men deployed either side of the gate, their rifles pointing at the house.

'You inside!' The lieutenant slung the M17 by the carrying strap as he cupped both hands to his mouth. 'Open this gate!'

There was a long silence, then the door facing the gate opened and an old man came out. He was tall and whipcord thin, with the bandied legs of a man more accustomed to horseback riding than vehicular traffic. His skin was tanned a deep, leathery brown, the face seamed like a contour map. His hair was pure silver, hanging ragged over jug-handle ears, as though he cut it himself with a knife. Chance wondered if he was part-Indian, because his nose was large and hooked, between flat cheekbones, and his eyes were the colour of jet, undimmed by age. He wore faded levis and an equally faded denim shirt. There was a venerable Winchester 30-30 cradled casually in his arms.

'You're trespassin'.' His voice was a lazy, Texas drawl. 'Get off my land an' quit botherin' my cows.'

Bergstrom looked taken aback.

'Get this gate open,' he repeated.

'No,' said the old man. And spat expressively.

'That's an order!' Bergstrom's face reddened. 'I'm Lieutenant Bergstrom of the Army of Texas.'

'Army of Texas?' Chance heard contempt in the reply. 'Goddam rabble of no-good bandits.'

Bergstrom's flush deepened.

'I've got direct orders from the President,' he warned.

'Garth Chambers?' The old man showed yellowed teeth as he sneered. 'I knew Garth when he was peddlin' his ass around the Senate in return for favours. Guess he ain't changed much.'

Chance grinned, liking the old man.

Bergstrom unshipped the M17 and snapped the safety off.

'I got orders to take this place over,' he shouted, anger

lending an almost hysterical edge to his voice. 'You don't open this goddam gate, I'll order my men to open fire.'

'Go ahead.' The old man shrugged eloquently. 'Won't do you no good. This place was built to take a bombing.'

'Fire!' Bergstrom screamed.

The old man moved back inside the building with surprising speed. The door slammed shut. 5.56mm bullets rattled off the walls and door. Chance saw that the windows were protected by steel shutters, and wondered exactly what the place was.

'Cease fire!' Bergstrom saw the uselessness of the attack. 'We'll go over the fence.'

'I wouldn't,' Chance called.

The lieutenant spun to glower at him, face suffused with rage and embarrassment.

'Why the hell not?'

Chance pointed at the small, rectangular boxes welded to the uprights inside the fence.

'It's electrified. The way that place is built, I'd take a bet there's enough power to fry a man.'

'Coming from where?' snarled Bergstrom. 'Only the city has power.'

Chance pointed to the windmills and the slab-like structure below.

'Windpower. And I'll bet there's an auxiliary generator somewhere, too.'

'God damn it to hell!' Bergstrom's knuckles went white as he clutched his rifle. 'Goddam old bastard!'

'The cannon could do it.' Chance jabbed a thumb towards the three-barrel cannon protruding from the nose of the Cobra. 'But it wouldn't be any use against that door. Or the walls.'

Bergstrom looked tempted for a moment, then he shook his head reluctantly.

'No. The President wants the whole place intact.'

'Why?' Chance asked. 'What use is it?'

Bergstrom studied his face for a moment, then: 'A forward base. The damn' place is a bomb shelter. We can cover the border from here a whole lot easier than from Austin.'

'You can cover the border with air patrols,' Chance suggested.

Then grinned as the lieutenant shook his head ruefully and said, 'No we can't. We don't have enough aviation fuel.'

'I'll be damned.' The grin faded from Chance's face. 'You mean those aircraft sitting out there don't fly?'

'They work all right,' Bergstrom countered. 'But we only got enough fuel for special missions.'

'Like this one?' Chance gestured at the house.

'That's right,' Bergstrom nodded. 'We were hoping to take it without too much trouble.'

'How'd you know about it?' Chance asked.

'A rumour and a map,' grunted Bergstrom enigmatically. 'That's all I know.'

'Well.' Chance sank his hands deep in his pockets, his face thoughtful. 'Looks like you got a problem.'

Bergstrom nodded. 'All right, let's get the hell back.'

'Nossir! Totally abortive.'

Bergstrom stood at rigid attention before Chambers' desk. On the far side of the mahogany expanse the President of Texas toyed with an ornate letter knife.

'You mean,' he said slowly, 'that you were stood off by an old man with a Winchester?'

'Sir!' There was a note of apology in Bergstrom's voice. 'The building is a fortress. You ordered it taken without damage.'

'Not possible.' Chance spoke from the side of the room, lounging against the bookshelves. 'The lieutenant's right, Garth.'

Chambers looked affronted at the casual use of his

Christian name. He fixed his baby-blue eyes on Chance's face, then turned back to Bergstrom.

'All right, Lieutenant. Dismissed.'

'Sir!' Bergstrom snapped off a neat salute and spun on his polished heels. As he marched away, he caught Chance's eye. He looked grateful.

The grey-haired man prepared to leave, but a gesture from the President halted him.

'I want to talk to you,' Chambers said. 'I need advice.'

'I need information,' Chance countered.

Chambers smiled placatingly and said, 'I'm doing my best to locate Stephanie. For God's sake, man! Don't you think I want to find her, too? She's my only child.'

'You told me California.' Chance's face got hard. 'But you don't have radio links with California. And you don't have the fuel to fly there.'

'Who told you that?' Chambers' face got angry. 'Bergstrom? I'll have his pips.'

'I'd have found out anyway,' Chance shrugged. 'Hell! If you can't fly border patrols, then you can't reach the coast.'

'It's a matter of time.' Chambers contained his anger. 'We'll have production started again before long.'

'Meanwhile you're isolated.' Chance gestured at the Texas flag. 'You're a big frog in a little pond, Garth. You want to extend your kingdom. Isn't that one of the reasons you want that bunker intact?'

Chambers nodded slowly, then smiled again.

'You always did think things through, Matthew. That place is a fortress. From the information I've received, it's one of the safest places in Texas. With that under my control, I could station men there and hold the entire Mexican border. I'd control all of South Texas.'

Chance grinned some more as enlightenment hit him.

'It is a small kingdom, isn't it?' he demanded softly.

'You're not a president, you're a warlord looking for more territory.'

'Unifying a state plunged into chaos,' snapped the balding man. 'Someone has to do it.'

Chance laughed out loud.

'I'll grant you one thing, Garth. You do think big.'

'And I can help you,' said Chambers. 'Listen, I don't intend to tell you how, but I can get word from the coast. I'll give you my word that I'll do everything I can to locate Stephanie and my grandchildren if you'll agree to help me.'

'And if I don't?' Chance asked, knowing the answer.

'The chain-gang.'

'And if I agree, and you succeed?'

Chambers eased back in his big chair, studying his son-in-law's hard face.

'Then you're free to go. I'll give you transport and provisions.'

'How long does this take?' Chance asked.

'A few months,' Chambers shrugged. 'Maybe longer. But I'll sweeten my offer – you help take that bunker and you can leave as soon as it's secured. I'll give you what information I can. You decide if you want to stay around.'

Chance didn't trust him, but with the chain-gang as his only alternative, he didn't really have much choice.

He nodded: 'All right. You got a deal.'

'Excellent.' The President favoured him with a beaming smile that was totally false. 'Now tell me how to capture the place. Intact.'

'That's the problem.' Chance hauled a chair closer to the desk and sat down. 'You can take out the fence with explosives. And it can be repaired easily enough. The building is something else. You had any penetration bombs, I could drop one through the roof. But I'd need the Thunderbolt for that.'

Chambers shook his head, smiling.

'Anyway,' Chance continued, 'that'd tear up the inside. Artillery could probably take the door out, but you'd still get internal damage. And you could find that door hard to replace – the way it looked, and from what you've said, I'd guess it's bomb-proof. Most likely molybdenum.'

Chambers frowned. 'So far, you're telling me what can't be done. What about a surprise attack?'

'Difficult.' Chance scratched at his chin, thinking he needed a shave. 'The ridge curves round from the southwest to the east and the house is built back into the north wall. The slope's steeper there, and on the far side it turns into a cliff. I could drop men on top, but that'd mean a ferry service. And even then they'd need to work down to get close.

'I fly in any other way, and he'll hear the chopper coming. In fact, if you use choppers at all, you've got to use up fuel. How're you fixed for ground transport and gasoline?'

'There's plenty,' Chambers replied. 'This is Texas.'

'How many men can you spare?' asked Chance. 'For a long-term operation?'

'Thirty,' was the answer. 'No more. Why?'

'Because we're talking about a siege,' grunted Chance.

Chapter Nine

It was a ragtag column that quit the city the following day.

Bergstrom and Chance led the way in a modified Jeep. Behind them came two Armoured Personnel Carriers, each holding ten troopers in addition to the two-man crews. Then there were two Dodge trucks, loaded with fuel and ordnance, two men in each. The APCs were armed with 0.5in Browning machineguns and the soldiers were equipped with M16s and 17s. Chance's M18 had been returned to him and now it sat in the carrying rack on his left side. Bergstrom was in the passenger seat, holding onto his M17.

'I want to thank you,' he said.

'For what?' Chance kept his eyes on the road, steering around the stalled vehicles.

'For getting me off the hook.' The lieutenant shrugged in embarrassment. 'The President doesn't like failure.'

'No,' Chance grinned. 'That's for sure. But you're not off it yet.'

'What d'you mean?' Bergstrom looked confused.

'Like we both know,' grunted Chance. 'That place is a fort. And we're supposed to take it with this shit.'

He ducked his head back to indicate the column. Bergstrom frowned.

'Then why'd you agree to try it?' he asked.

'I like fresh air,' grinned Chance.

Bergstrom stared at him without saying anything and Chance took their speed up a little as the road ahead cleared. They were on the outskirts of the city now and their surroundings resembled a bomb site. Rubble filled most of the side roads, the buildings reduced to ruins that seldom stood more than waist high. Weeds were reclaiming the desolation, spreading resolutely over the shattered walls and fallen roofs. Nothing moved: it was wasteland.

'Urban reclamation?' Chance asked cynically.

'Re-organization.' Bergstrom said it straight-faced. 'Most of the places were empty. Vermin was taking over.'

'Animal or human?' Chance kept his voice even.

'Both.' The lieutenant gestured around them. 'We don't have enough men to administer the entire city, so the President decided to pull back on the centre. We seeded all this with poison to clear out the animals.'

'What happened to the people?' Chance asked. 'They go, too?'

'There was some fighting with the dissidents.' Bergstrom's voice was earnest. 'But like I said, most of these places were empty, anyway. There were too many predators, so the inhabitants moved towards the centre.'

'How do they live?' wondered the grey-haired man.

'They work.' Bergstrom ran a hand through his tidily-clipped blond hair. 'Everyone works.'

So far as Chance had seen, that meant either in the armed forces or on the chain-gangs. Garth Chambers had built himself a military hierarchy that didn't seem to have very much to do with democracy or freedom, but an awful lot to do with power. And, he thought, good ole Garth is suckering everyone along. Bergstrom believes in it and the others just do what they're told. Not really surprising if the alternatives are the chain-gang or the cross. Yeah, Garth has really got himself a new toy to play with.

He felt a sudden surge of raw hate for the old man. It had been Chambers who turned Stephanie against him. All right, it hadn't been easy getting the airline started after his combat tour was up and he walked out of the Marines. And Steph had always been accustomed to luxury: she never had properly understood why he consistently refused her daddy's offers of a position with one of his companies. Nor had she agreed with him about the coming collapse. Daddy said things were going to be all right; and if they weren't, then there was always Daddy to fall back on. So she had scorned his trips into the Maine wilderness, determined to hone the skills he had learned in the Marines into real survival training.

Then one day he had come back from seven days living off the land to find her gone. No word. No note. Nothing. He had allowed sufficient time to pass for a flight to reach Texas, then called the Chambers' home. Garth had taken the call. He had told Chance that his wife had left him, finally giving up on his craziness and their semi-poverty. Chance had argued. Chambers had told him there was no point pursuing the matter: Stephanie had had enough and there was a divorce arranged. The Chambers' lawyers were handling it; and if Chance was foolish enough to try to contact his wife, then Chambers would see to it that he spent some time behind bars. It could be arranged easily enough.

Chance had known it was true: Garth Chambers wielded sufficient power to manipulate the law. Sufficient to close down the airline. He had called a few more times; cabled; written letters. Twice, he had lost his bonus on delivery flights by detouring to land in Austin and attempt a physical confrontation. Armed guards had turned him away from the ranch-house and heavily-built 'Personnel Officials' from the Chambers Building. Then the divorce had come through, awarding custody of David and Jennifer to Steph. The next day, nursing a bad hang-over, he had received a brief note from his ex-wife. It had said simply that she felt this was for the best and she was taking the children to a meditation centre to get her head clear.

That had come close to finishing him. He was drunk for three days, leaving the flying to his partner. Then Warren, having logged far too many hours in the air without sleep, flew the Beechcraft into a mountainside. Chance had sobered up fast. He pulled himself together and sold the business. Sent Warren's share to his parents. There was word that a survey team was looking for a reliable pilot to ferry supplies and personnel to the French scientific research stations spread around the Southern Indian Ocean.

That had seemed far enough away and he had taken the post. The pay was lousy, but the work was hard enough he got too tired to brood. And when the holocaust he had foreseen came, he had been safe.

Until he came back home looking for the people he loved.

Yeah, he thought. Garth has a lot to answer for. And he will. Once I've got the information I need.

The rubble faded behind them and the convoy pushed into desert country. As Bergstrom had told him, there was little sign of the mutant creatures produced by the nuclear drift and the chemical weapons. Occasionally they saw spider webs, and once a gila monster hissed at them from the shadow of a ravine, but mostly there was nothing except the sand and the undergrowth.

They kept moving until a little before noon, then Bergstrom ordered a halt. The APCs rolled to a stop and the men inside clambered out with sweat on their faces and a chorus of complaints.

'Be best if we travelled by night,' Chance suggested. 'Those men are gonna get dehydrated.'

'No way!' Bergstrom said it too fast.

'Why the hell not?' queried Chance. 'The APCs got infra-red drive lights and the rest of us got headlights.'

'Too dangerous. The road's not safe.'

Before Chance could question him further, the officer turned away, going over to the men. Chance watched, frowning as he wondered how much Bergstrom was holding back. With the kind of equipment they were carrying, there would be no difficulty spotting their path. So why was it dangerous? He began to wonder how far the influence of Chambers' control extended. Maybe not so far as the old bastard wanted him to believe.

He sipped a little water and hunkered down by the Jeep to eat his rations.

They were tasteless as ever and he was glad when Bergstrom decided they should start off again.

He watched the reluctant troopers file back inside the APCs and climbed into the Jeep. Bergstrom waved an arm and bellowed 'Forwards' like something out of an old movie and the roar of the two big General Motors six-cylinder diesels drowned out the smoother start of the two trucks. Chance put the Jeep in gear and led off with the lieutenant checking his map. It showed a route to the block-house that was both manageable, and that avoided radiation pockets. Chance and Bergstrom had studied it together, calculating the time it would take them to reach their objective.

Allowing for detours and overland travel, Chance didn't give them more than a 20mph average speed, which meant two clear days. He still didn't know why Bergstrom refused to travel by night, but if his guess about unexpected – or, in the lieutenant's case, expected – dangers was correct, then it looked as though Garth Chambers' 'Republic' extended no more than a day's travel southwest of Austin. The border markers he had seen coming into Texas had been west of Houston, so it began to look as though Chambers' influence might be limited to a central strip.

Innocently, he asked Bergstrom: 'How far do your patrols go northwards?'

Bergstrom glanced at him, then shrugged.

'About midway to Dallas. Like I told you – there's too much radiation up there.'

'West?' Chance asked casually.

And Bergstrom replied, 'As far as Abilene.'

Chance nodded, his suspicions confirmed: Garth Chambers ruled a strip running through the centre of what was left of Texas. It was maybe 40,000 square miles, the borders tenuous. He needed the block-house to extend his domain. He had spoken of controlling the Mexican border, but now Chance began to wonder if there weren't other warlords. Maybe in San Antonio or Corpus Christi: he had only the word of Chambers and his minions that no other cities had survived intact.

He kept his thoughts to himself as he drove on through the burning afternoon.

On his suggestion, they halted twice to let the men in the APCs stretch their legs and drink a little water from the tanks carried on the trucks. Then, as night approached, Bergstrom called a halt.

'We got at least another thirty minutes of good light.' Chance glanced up at the sky. 'Let's push on.'

'No.' The lieutenant shook his head, his voice definite. 'We bivouac here. It's a good place.'

Chance looked around and shrugged: it seemed no better than the country ahead. It was flat, mostly sand except where cholla and chaparral showed a greyish green. There were giant saguarro thrusting skeletal limbs from the landscape, and over to the east he could see a thick stand of mesquite. Bergstrom was already yelling orders, and the vehicles were rolling slowly into a protective circle that again reminded Chance of an old Western movie. Perimeter guards were posted and rations taken from the supply trucks. The sun began to fade behind the western horizon and the empty terrain was lit with ethereal pink light. Then, abruptly, it was gone and the sky was a velvet blue pricked through with stars. Very faintly, in three different places, Chance could see the glow of radiation pockets. The temperature dropped as suddenly as the sun and Chance suggested cutting mesquite to start a fire.

'No fires!' Bergstrom snapped his refusal in a nervous voice that he then tried to hide. 'Standing Orders on patrol duty.'

He turned away, leaving Chance to wonder what he was so worried about. The grey-haired man saw that he would get no explanation and squatted beside the Jeep, checking his rifle by touch. Bergstrom's obvious nerviness was beginning to communicate: if the man was so damn' jumpy, there had to be a reason for it. And Chance wanted to be ready if the reason showed. He checked his clip was loaded on the full thirty rounds and dropped an extra into the deep side pocket of his combat pants.

The night was silent. Even the breeze that usually came with the setting of the sun failed to rustle the undergrowth. Chance ambled casually around the tight circle of vehicles, staring at the desert. It was still. There was nothing moving. Without trying to question anyone further, he returned to the Jeep and spread his bedroll. He stretched out with the M18 cradled in his arms, right hand on the pistol grip.

Soon he was asleep.

Not long after, the attack came.

Chapter Ten

The sounds of dying woke him.

They were soft, whispery sounds that ended with faint, almost soggy thuds. He was instantly alert, shifting off his bedroll to flatten alongside the Jeep as he thumbed the safety down and grasped the M18 in both hands. The others became aware of the attack as Chance realized what the sounds were. A perimeter guard loosed off a random burst, then screamed, staggering back as he dropped his rifle to press both hands against his throat. He moved to the centre of the bivouac, his screaming dropping to a strangled gurgling sound, and abruptly slumped to a squatting position. His hands fell away from his throat and he tilted slowly sideways as his choking died away. Chance saw the cross bow bolt protruding from his neck and peered under the Jeep.

The luminous hands of his Rolex showed it was a little after 4 A.M.: a good time to mount a sneak attack. The stars had faded behind an overlay of cloud and the surrounding flat was shrouded in darkness. The guards would be bored, their concentration lessened. And the rest of the convoy would have been asleep.

Now they were all awake. Except the four men stretched on the sand with crossbow shafts jutting from their skulls and throats. Panicky fire was lighting up the shadows, the early morning noisy with the thunder of the big Browning machineguns mounted on the APCs and the more staccato rattle of the smaller calibre rifles.

Chance flattened against the cold ground, trying to outline the attackers against the sky. He could see nothing, but the bulk of the attack – judging by the direction of the crossbow bolts – was coming from the direction of the mesquite. He eased back, looking for Bergstrom.

The lieutenant was crouched by the nearest APC, M17 at his shoulder. He started as Chance came up behind him.

'Listen.' The grey-haired man shouted over the roar of the guns. 'You got tracer or phosphorous?'

Bergstrom looked blank, then nodded.

'For the Brownings.'

'Good.' Chance clutched the officer's shoulder, hauling him round. 'Load one and stand the gunner down. I'll take it.'

His voice was commanding and Bergstrom moved to obey without question. He scuttled down the side of the APC and clambered into the gunner's cabin. Seconds later, the Browning fell silent and Bergstrom reappeared. There was a pause, then the gunner jumped to the ground. His face was pale and Chance saw panic in his eyes as he stood, staring desperately around him. Then he screamed as a bolt took him in the left eye. His head was jerked round by the impact so that his face was in profile, the shaft protruding either side of his skull. With brutally professional indifference, Chance noted that it was a twelve-inch length of smooth wood, flighted with what looked like plastic and tipped with a vicious head of beaten metal. The gunner collapsed in a loose-limbed heap and Chance climbed into the cab.

He settled in the bucket seat and grabbed the firing grip. Sighting on the mesquite, he held the trigger down, traversing the long barrel across the thicket. Flame gusted from the muzzle, blinding him momentarily. Then, as his vision adjusted, he saw the long lines of fire pierce the night, seeming to link him with the bushes.

Where the bullets hit, flame began to sparkle. He swung his sights back over the mesquite, his mouth tight as the heavy gun shuddered in his hands. More flame burst from the sun-dried wood, so that a series of small fires started. They began to join as Chance continued to traverse the Browning. Suddenly the entire thicket erupted in flame.

Chance brought the gun around to the left and sent a long line of phosphorous shells screaming over the undergrowth either side of the thicket. Flame tongued skywards as a brushfire started. Figures leapt from the fire, screaming and burning as the incandescent bullets transformed them to blazing scarecrows.

The Browning snapped empty. Chance looked for a fresh ammo box. He could see none, so he swung down from the APC and grabbed his rifle.

There were men between the flames and the bivouac now. Most were running in panic, but a few were charging the parked vehicles, their shouting combining with the crackle of the bushfire and the rattle of the defenders' guns. Chance grinned his approval as he saw that Bergstrom had ordered the APC on the far side of the circle loaded with tracer, so that a ring of fire surrounded the vehicles. The few remaining attackers were easy targets and only a handful got close enough to be really dangerous.

One was headed directly for Chance's position. With the fire behind him, it was easy to see why they had been so difficult to spot. He was dressed entirely in black. A loose, black tunic covered his torso and arms; baggy black pants, his legs. His feet were swathed in black rags, and a black hood covered his head. There was a knife long enough that it was almost a short sword sheathed on his belt and an axe in his hands. Chance snapped the M18 to single-shot fire and aimed almost casually at the man's chest. The rifle barked once and the man's forwards charge halted as the impact counteracted his momentum. The axe dropped from his upraised hands and he took two faltering steps onwards, then crashed face-down.

Chance looked along the line of flames.

There were no more attackers moving.

Only bodies.

He remained crouched under the cover of the APC until he was sure the ambush was finished, then eased cautiously to his feet. He turned to see Bergstrom wiping sweat from his forehead and went over to the lieutenant. The officer's face was a mixture of relief and loathing.

'You want to tell me now?' Chance snarled. 'They're the reason you wouldn't travel by night?'

Bergstrom nodded. 'They'd have picked us off. One by one.'

'Who are they?' Chance demanded.

'Nightmen.' Bergstrom shuddered, unable to conceal his distaste. 'They live out here.'

'Yeah.' Chance grinned tightly. 'So the Republic isn't as in control as Garth said.'

'They're bandits.' Bergstrom defended his leader. 'We're destroying them.'

'They damn' nearly destroyed us,' Chance grated. Then, curious: 'Why do you call them Nightmen?'

'They only operate by night,' Bergstrom replied. 'They're scavengers. Mutants. They live mostly around the radiation pits.'

Chance grunted and turned away. He was interested in the lieutenant's reluctance to inform him of an obvious danger. Like the vagueness about the exact limits of the new Republic, it suggested hidden weakness in Chambers' power structure.

He moved out between the APC and the truck ahead, holding the M18 ready to use. The fire was still burning, but it was fading away as the undergrowth was consumed. He glanced at the Rolex and saw the attack had lasted over an hour. Dawn was not far off now, the chill rebated by the heat of the flames. He halted a few feet from the body of the man he had shot and studied it for a while. It was not quite right: the arms were a little too long and the legs a little too short. The shoulders were massive, and the back was humped, thrusting the head forwards so that there was no evidence of a neck. The axe the man had carried was a piece of steel beaten into shape and sharpened on a cold forge. It was set on a long pole of some hard wood, held in place by rawhide thongs.

He went up close and saw the bloody exit hole where his shot had emerged from the back, at the base of the hump. Still pointing the rifle at the corpse, he kicked it hard in the ribs. It didn't move, so he turned it over and yanked the hood away. From the deformity of the body, and Bergstrom's obvious loathing, he had anticipated ugliness, some monstrous face. Instead, he found himself looking down at the features of a damned angel. A mane of wavy golden hair framed perfect looks, marred only by the snarl fixed forever on the well-formed lips. The eyes were wide open, staring sightlessly back at him with a clear blue intensity. The face might have belonged to a film star, and it sat incongruously on the grotesquery of the body.

Frowning, he approached a second corpse. He didn't bother examining its abnormalities, but picked up the crossbow it still held.

He examined it in the glow of the smouldering brush: a Lindstrom, deadly over around 500 yards. They had used them in the Marine Combat Force for silent killing at long range.

Moving on to the other corpses, he saw that they all carried a mixture of factory manufactured and home-made weapons. They were all clad in black, and all deformed. Three were women. He looked around, nostrils crinkling as a breeze started to blow the acrid reek of the burning undergrowth and the sweeter odour of roasted flesh towards him. It reminded him of the past, and he strode abruptly back towards the vehicles.

Bergstrom met him on the perimeter, his youthful face smeared with soot and lined with worry.

'We lost nine men,' he said. 'And one truck's useless.'

Chance nodded tersely. 'All right, so there's room in the APCs for baggage. Will they attack again?'

'I don't know.' Bergstrom shook his head. 'We don't even know how many there are.'

Chance grinned: there were more chinks appearing in Garth Chambers' armour.

'What do you know about them?' he demanded.

'Oh, hell!' Bergstrom looked anguished. 'It's supposed to be privileged information.'

'The hell it is!' Chance's face got ugly. Suddenly the M18 was pressed up against Bergstrom's midriff. 'I have to fight, I want to know who. Or what.'

His voice was low and harsh, pitched so that only Bergstrom could hear him. The lieutenant stared at him: he could read death in Chance's eyes. He glanced nervously over his shoulder, as though afraid of being overheard. The nearest troopers were several yards away, bandaging wounds or peering warily at the dying brushfire. He shrugged and nodded:

'All right. I guess you're entitled. After the bombings we got a lot of freaks appearing. The President decided the only way to keep the Republic clean was to drive them out or kill them. We killed some, but most got away into the desert. They weren't any real problem at first, but then they started to join up in groups. They got some kind of crazy religion that worships the radiation, so they group around the pits. It affects them somehow so that they can't stand sunlight. That's why we call them the Nightmen.

'We got no idea how many there are. Hell! We don't even know if they're capable of breeding.'

'How come?' Chance was suspicious. 'You could send a column against one of the pits.'

'We did.' Bergstrom's voice was bitter. 'We lost eighty men and three assault vehicles.'

'The helicopters,' Chance suggested. 'You try them?'

'Would you fly over one of those pits?' Bergstrom countered. 'Close enough to spot the core?'

'No,' Chance admitted, shaking his head. 'I wouldn't.'

'That's why we don't know much about them.' The lieutenant looked down at the rifle barrel touching his stomach. 'So what do we do now?'

Chance eased the M18 away. 'We roll,' he said. 'Fast.'

Bergstrom nodded. 'I'll get the equipment stowed.'

He spun round, once again assuming an officer's purposeful stance as he barked orders at his men. Chance lounged against the Jeep, checking his rifle as he thought about Bergstrom's words.

Chambers appeared to have adopted a Nazi-like attitude that was back-firing badly. His control was now obviously far less firm than he had given Chance to understand. His borders were closer – and less secure – than he suggested, and he was suffering problems from within. If the Nightmen could account for eighty soldiers armed with modern weapons there had to be an awful lot of them. And organized, too. Maybe even enough, with enough organization, to pose a real threat to the President's power.

And there was still the old man in the block-house.

Speaking with him could prove interesting: if the place had been designed as a bomb shelter, then it would almost certainly be equipped with radio facilities. If the opportunity came up, then Chance would take it.

He looked up as Bergstrom approached.

'We're ready to move.'

'Good.' Chance climbed into the passenger seat of the Jeep. 'You drive.'

* * *

The initial greyness of the dawn was augmented by the pall of smoke drifting from the brush behind them. The breeze came out of the north, tailing them as they moved southwest so that the pungency of the air served as a reminder of their danger. Chance looked back as a dull explosion echoed through the acrid morning. A column of new flame jetted from the damaged truck as the charges Bergstrom had planted tore the Dodge apart.

'At least they won't use the metal,' grinned the lieutenant.

Chance nodded his approval and went back to surveying the terrain ahead.

The flat was shrouded in grey, dew glistening on the saguarro and the chaparral. Then crimson suffused the eastern horizon and the sun drifted slowly into view. Where it rose, the crimson became gold, spreading resolutely across the sky in an ever-widening dome that pushed the light steadily farther west. Suddenly it was morning. Chance almost expected to hear birdsong, but the desert remained silent and still. It felt menacing.

He scanned the way ahead, and saw that the flatlands broke up into a series of low switchbacks. Over to the west the switchbacks grew to solid ridges that undulated towards the horizon like frozen waves. Eastwards, the land was flat.

He held the M18 ready to fire. The switchbacks looked like a good place for an ambush.

Chapter Eleven

'Halt!'

Chance's command brought an instant reaction from Bergstrom. The Jeep skidded to a stop, and behind them the first APC, the remaining Dodge, and the second APC applied their brakes.

'How far do they go from the pits?' Chance studied the map, locating the radiation sites.

'I don't know.' Bergstrom's voice was earnest. 'No one knows.'

Chance grunted, standing up to study the switchbacks better. He reached for the lieutenant's binoculars, adjusting the individual focus of the Nikon lenses. Beyond the undulations, the country climbed steeper, then became heavily ridged. The Nightmen appeared to lack transport, so it was unlikely they could have reached the badlands by now. But the switchbacks were dangerous. The bottoms were invisible, and a small army could be hiding behind the scarps. He set the binoculars back in their case and dropped into the seat.

'What now?' asked Bergstrom.

'Scout ahead.' Chance pointed at the broken ground. 'There could be an ambush. So we take the Jeep up to have a look. The others stay here.'

'I'll give the order.' Bergstrom climbed from the Jeep.

Chance noticed that he took the keys with him.

The grey-haired man remained in the passenger seat as the lieutenant issued the command to halt and wait. He glanced at the fuel gauge and saw that the tank was close to full. There was a two gallon water tank strapped to the tail, and the rear of the vehicle held ration packs and an ammo box containing seven clips.

It was sufficient for what he had in mind.

He waited for Bergstrom to return, staring at the terrain as the officer settled in the drive seat.

'Take it slow,' he cautioned as Bergstrom started the Jeep again. 'Those crossbows got a range of about five hundred yards, so haul up six hundred out from that first dip.'

Bergstrom nodded, acknowledging Chance's authority, and held the Jeep down to around twenty miles an hour as they rolled towards the nearest switchback.

The ground rose slightly as they got closer, obscuring the view beyond. Chance tapped Bergstrom on the shoulder, indicating he should stop, and said: 'I'll check it on foot. Wait here.'

Before the officer could agree or object, Chance was out of the Jeep and moving at a lope towards the ridge. He held the M18 across his chest, right hand clutching the pistol grip and the safety off, set to rapid fire. A few yards from the crest – before his head could show on the far side – he dropped flat on his belly and began to crawl up the slope. The rim was wind-scoured, devoid of vegetation, so he moved laterally towards a slight dip that would leave him less exposed than a direct approach.

He eased his head warily over the rim and saw empty ground ahead. The trough between the first switchback and the next was a hundred-foot avenue of cholla-dotted sand that ran more or less straight on an east-west line. Chance went over the top in a rolling dive, letting the slope take him down until he touched bottom and came up on his feet, running for the far side. He went up the incline and flattened again below the next rim. The trough there was empty. He repeated the roll-and-run process to check out the trough between the second and third switchbacks and found no sign of danger. Looking back, he saw that the first incline hid both the Jeep and the waiting column. He grinned and began to run back to the nervous Bergstrom.

'It's clear as best I could tell,' he announced. 'But we'd better take the Jeep in deeper before the convoy moves up.'

Bergstrom nodded and engaged the four-wheel drive, sending the Jeep up the slope.

'How far in did you go?' he asked.

'Three ridges.' Chance grabbed for a handhold as the wheels spun on loose sand, slewing the Jeep round. 'Let's go deeper.'

Bergstrom grunted an affirmative and corrected the skid, taking the Jeep fast over the next rim. The sun was climbing towards its zenith by now and the desert baked in the heat. Haze shimmered around them, combining with the undulations of the terrain to obscure the convoy still waiting a quarter mile back. They crossed five switchbacks without seeing signs of life of any kind, then Bergstrom halted.

'There's no ambush,' he said, relief in his voice.

'You want to bet?'

Chance brought the M18 across his chest so that the muzzle was touching Bergstrom's temple. The lieutenant gasped in surprise and began to turn his head. The pressure of the rifle halted the movement.

'Climb out slowly,' Chance ordered. 'I don't want to kill you.'

Bergstrom's eyes flickered nervously towards his own rifle. Chance pressed the M18 harder against his skull. The officer eased his left foot clear of the vehicle, his head turning so that the muzzle of the M18 was pointed directly between his eyes. He was awkward as he climbed onto the sand, backing out of the Jeep as Chance slid across the seats holding the rifle one-handed.

He lowered his aim so that the muzzle was pointed at Bergstrom's stomach and gestured at the Detonics .45 holstered on the Army belt.

'Take that out left-handed and throw it.'

Bergstrom's face was pale, a mixture of fear and anger and confusion showing in his eyes. 'What is this?' he asked as he tossed the automatic pistol onto the sand.

'I guess you'd call it a hi-jack,' Chance grinned. 'I'd call it escape.'

'You're crazy.' Bergstrom's voice was harsh, coming out of a dry mouth. 'You'll never make it.'

'I made it this far.' Chance went on grinning. 'I think I can go some farther.'

Bergstrom stared at him as though contemplating an attack. Chance put his left hand on the forward grip of the rifle.

'You're not a bad kid,' he murmured, 'but you're pretty damn' misguided. Garth Chambers is just an old man hungry for whatever power he can grab. You're crazy following him.'

Bergstrom's jaw tightened, his lips curling in a snarl. Chance lifted his right hand from the M18's pistol grip to the neck of the shoulder stock. The movement was so fast Bergstrom's right foot was still shifting forwards as the butt swung up and round. It caught the lieutenant on the point of his chin, slamming his head back as his teeth snapped hard together. His eyes glazed and he stepped backwards. Chance reversed the swing as he moved closer, driving the flat of the stock against the side of Bergstrom's neck. The shock paralyzed the younger man, jerking his body rigid so that for an instant he appeared to stand to attention. Then his knees folded and he collapsed limp onto the sand. Chance lowered the safety catch of the rifle to the *on* position and knelt beside the officer. Bergstrom was still breathing, so Chance trotted down the slope to retrieve the Detonics .45 automatic. He climbed back towards the Jeep working the slide to empty the magazine. Then he dropped the automatic beside the unconscious man and climbed back in the vehicle.

Tossing Bergstrom's M17 into the back, he set his own

rifle in the clips beside the drive seat. Then he started the Jeep and headed into the badlands. Bergstrom would be out for thirty minutes or more, and then he faced at least an hour's walking before he could reach the convoy. By then, Chance would have a head start. Better if the officer still refused to travel by night.

The grey-haired man began to whistle softly as he built up speed.

By mid-afternoon the landscape had become broken enough that Chance was forced to slow down. The switchbacks had given way to the steeper ridges, and these were interlaced with gulleys that occasionally dropped away too steeply for even the Jeep to negotiate. Several times he was forced to detour from the course marked on Bergstrom's map, running along dry river beds or stony gulches before finding a suitable route towards his objective. Using the Nikon binoculars at full range he could now make out the line of bluffs he calculated hid the block-house. They were a dark blur in the heat haze, and he estimated it would take the remainder of the day and part of the night before he reached them. Checking the map, he saw that two radiation pits were marked either side of his course; one lay about five miles ahead and to his left, the other, around fifteen miles out to his right. Both were too close for his liking, and he debated the merits of driving through the night or waiting for daylight.

The way the terrain looked, he could leave the left-hand pit behind him before darkness fell, but that would put him close to the other at the most dangerous time. He glanced at his Rolex: it was 3.10 P.M. At least five more hours of good light.

He decided to push on.

The sun moved slowly across the sky, shadows lengthening as dusk approached. Chance halted around six o'clock to drink water and open a pack of rations. He had covered less ground than he hoped, but that meant Bergstrom's pursuit – if the lieutenant decided to come after him – would be slowed even more. It also meant that he would pass within ten miles of the second radiation pit some time before midnight – unless he stayed put for the night.

Cursing his lack of information, he wondered how far out the Nightmen ranged, and if they had any kind of advance warning system. There was no way of knowing, and now the bluffs were within striking distance: he made up his mind to keep moving.

It was a decision made calmly, utilising all the facts at his disposal. Which were not really many. He knew the Nightmen could move silently, and as they had become nocturnal they presumably had good night vision. If they had spotted him – or if they ranged far enough from the pits – they could attack in the dark and possibly disable the Jeep. A moving target would be harder to hit. And it should be possible to outrun them.

He checked the loads in both rifles, placing the M17 on the floor at his feet. Then he found an unexpected bonus amongst the equipment in the bolt-down storage box – a flare gun. He loaded the stubby pistol and wedged it between the supports of the passenger seat, close to his right hip. There were twelve flares, and he dropped two into each of the chest-pockets of his shirt. Then, hoping he was making the right decision, he started the Jeep and continued towards the bluffs.

The badlands gave way to slightly easier terrain as the sun touched the western horizon. Chance increased his speed a little, using the last of the light to cover as much ground as possible. He estimated that he was now level with the radiation pit. And that it would take another two hours at least to get past and out of range.

The sun went down and the sky to the west was briefly

red. Then full dark settled and over to his right he could see the glow of the pit like some subterranean furnace throwing flame against the night. He cursed as he saw that it was a whole lot closer than the map indicated. Then chuckled cynically as he realized the faulty reference was another indication of Garth Chambers' inherent weakness. He switched on the headlights and turned the hood-mounted spotlight on the passenger side to beam brilliance over the desert to his right. If sunlight hurt the Nightmen's eyes, then maybe artificial light had the same effect.

He covered some seven miles without incident. Then, as he was climbing a slope towards a long ridge that curved away into the darkness, he heard something strike the Jeep's hood.

It made a metallic clatter and he guessed it was a crossbow bolt.

Then knew it as a second rattled off the left-side fender.

They were fired at maximum range, from the crest of the ridge. Which meant he was driving into the field of fire.

He hauled the wheel over, slewing the Jeep across the slope so that the headlights sent twin columns of radiance lancing through the night, bathing the crest in brilliance.

Two figures were outlined. They were standing up to gain maximum deflection for their crossbows and the headlights struck them full on. Chance heard them scream as they lifted their arms to cover their eyes, and then they were gone, scuttling for cover behind the rim. Chance held the Jeep in third gear, ignoring the whining protest of the engine as he steered one-handed. His right dropped to the flare gun, yanking the pistol from its resting place and thumbing the safety clear. The Jeep yawed towards the crest, the headlights burning into the sky. Chance pointed the flare gun forwards and slightly left and squeezed the trigger.

A streamer of sparks jetted through the night. Then a ball

of incandescent white fire erupted thirty feet above the sand. The Jeep lurched over the rim and Chance shoved the gear stick into fourth as he saw flat terrain ahead.

There were black-clad figures over to his left. Six or seven of them. All of them cowering beneath the flare's light. Chance put his foot hard against the gas pedal, still steering with his left hand as he snapped the flare pistol open and awkwardly worked the spent cartridge free. He shoved another into the breech and fired the pistol again, this time directly at the yelling figures.

The flare hit one of the Nightmen as he turned to run, sending him reeling back as brilliant scarlet gouted from his chest. The flare was imbedded in flesh, burning the man as it ignited so that his clothing took flame and he was transformed into a semi-human torch. He fell down on his back, screaming as he roasted, writhing over the sand so that his burning body cast wild patterns of light through the chaparral. Chance gunned the Jeep, re-loading the pistol and firing at random behind him. Again, brilliance turned the night into day. It came close to blinding Chance as he risked a glance at his rear-view mirror. Then it faded as the first flares burned out and the land took a downwards slant.

Chance held the Jeep at the fastest speed he dared as he went down the slope and hurtled up the far side, to where the ground flattened again. Saguarro showed in the headlights, and he felt cholla crush beneath the fender and the wheels. Something hit the rear of the passenger seat, and when he glanced sideways he saw a crossbow shaft jutting through the canvas.

There was shouting off to his right now, and he caught glimpses of Nightmen running through the brush, shading their eyes as they moved diagonally to head him off. He wondered how they hoped to outrun the Jeep. Then saw the reason as sudden blackness cut across the path of the lights.

It was a knife-cut through the flat: a ravine that ran in a

straight line directly across his path. The headlights showed the far edge some twenty feet from the vertical drop confronting him. He reacted with a speed born of pure instinct. Slamming the Jeep out of four-wheel drive into front-wheel, he snatched the hand-brake up. At the same time, he spun the steering wheel over to the left and jammed his foot down against the gas pedal. The engine screamed as it fought the brake for control of the vehicle. The rear wheels locked as the fronts spun against the sand. The Jeep lurched sideways, spinning halfway around its own length. The left-side wheels lifted from the ground, and for an instant Chance thought he had hurled himself into the ravine. Then the thing righted and he was racing at full speed alongside the cut.

Crossbow shafts whistled over his head and he heard the Nightmen howling their fury at his escape. Several bolts hit the Jeep, and he felt one rustle his hair, narrowly missing the upright windshield.

Then he was out of range, still running beside the barrier.

He kept moving until he felt confident the Nightmen were lost behind him, then slowed. There was no visual sign of any radiation in the immediate vicinity, so he halted the Jeep and began to check for damage.

There were two bolts jutting from the passenger seat and one – fired at maximum range – from the drive seat. The tyres were safe, but the canteen on the tail was punctured in four places: he was out of water. Wearily he climbed back into the vehicle and started off again. The ravine was not shown on Bergstrom's map, so he had no idea how far it extended, or where he could cross it. All he could do was continue to follow the edge until a place showed. Either that, or abandon the Jeep and attempt to climb down.

When he checked the depth of the fissure, he discarded the last idea. The ravine looked as though it might have been formed by an earthquake or a bomb. The bottom was shrouded in darkness and the sides glass-smooth. There were no handholds, and even using the towrope lashed to the rear fender, he had no way of climbing the far side.

He got back in the Jeep and drove on into the morning.

Chapter Twelve

Daylight revealed the full extent of his problem. The ravine stretched in an unbroken line in both directions, a seemingly impassable barrier. Staring back the way he had come, he guessed it was a natural fault line opened up by whatever explosion had created the radiation pit to the west. That meant there was probably a way around if he skirted the pit, but that would mean retracing his path and risking a second confrontation with the Nightmen. If he continued in an easterly direction, he had no idea how far he needed to travel before the fault closed up. Going back north would return him to Chambers' territory. And without water, he could dehydrate before he got anywhere.

There seemed only one choice that was at all valid: follow the ravine east and hope for a crossing point.

He started the Jeep and drove at an even 25mph to conserve fuel. The sun got higher, bathing the glassy walls of the fissure in golden light. Chance felt his mouth get dry, and thought about halting to find water-bearing cactus. No, he decided, best leave that for nightfall. While there was light the optimum for survival lay in pushing on.

He covered thirty-three miles before he saw a way.

Ahead, a low ridge ran out of the northeast to the edge of the ravine. It started a mile or more out on the flat, climbing at a shallow angle towards the cleft. Then it was split by the fissure, continuing in a southwesterly direction on the far side. It was slightly lower on the other side.

Chance took the Jeep up to the rim and climbed out. The ridge stood about twenty feet above the desert, and where it met the ravine it fell away in a sheer drop. At this point the ravine was no more than fifteen feet wide, the continuation of the ridge between five and ten feet lower.

It was a long shot.

But it looked like the only one he had.

He got back in the drive seat and took the Jeep down the slope a few hundred yards. Wind had scoured the surface and the sun had baked it hard: there was good traction. He swung the nose to point up the gradient, then revved the engine fiercely. The tachometer needle spun into the red and he pushed the gear stick into first. The Jeep strained forwards. He dropped the hand-brake and slammed the change into second as the vehicle lurched up the slope. As he switched to third gear he jammed the gas pedal all the way down.

The Jeep rocketed over the sand.

Fourth gear. And the edge was getting closer.

He clutched the steering wheel in both hands, teeth clenched as he willed the vehicle to perform.

Blue sky showed like a curtain before him. Windrush tore at his hair.

Then he was on the edge.

And the Jeep was leaving the ridge. Hurtling through the air with the engine screaming and the wheels spinning on nothing.

There was an instant of stomach-churning uncertainty as he seemed to hang above the cleft. He was vaguely aware of Bergstrom's rifle bouncing from the floor to tumble over and over into the darkness below. Then the far side of the ridge was rushing towards him and he knew he was going to pile nose-down into the vertical face. Follow the rifle into the pit.

Then the Jeep landed with a bone-jarring crash. Chance was lifted from the seat, his feet leaving the pedals, his arms strained as he clung to the wheel.

He came back down with a force that sent shock running

up his spine, a grunt bursting from his stretched lips as his teeth ground together. But he was over. The Jeep was rolling down the slope, the engine stalled. He set his feet on the pedals again and brought the engine back to life, following the line of the ridge to where he was able to rejoin the flatlands and swing the nose southwest.

He halted to consult the map and the compass mounted on the instrument panel. The bluffs were more west than south now, and he could see them clearly through the Nikon binoculars. He peered at the fuel gauge, doubting he had sufficient gasoline left to make the old man's stronghold. It didn't matter: he would cover as much ground as possible in the Jeep, then go in on foot.

What his reception might be, he would worry about later.

The gas ran out just before dusk settled over the desert. Chance was a mile out from the bluffs and thirst was making his mouth taste like the sand. He coaxed the engine a little farther then let it die. He didn't want to ruin the Jeep: he might need to come back to it. Leaving the keys in the ignition, he rummaged through the equipment stowed in the back. Using the towrope and his bedroll, he fashioned a crude sack. Into it he dropped an emergency medical kit and most of the ammo clips. The others he slid into his pockets, together with flares for the pistol tucked under his belt. There was no container that would carry water, so he reluctantly opened the drain valve on the radiator and swallowed a few mouthfuls of the foul-tasting water. Then he slung the sack on his back, picked up the M18, and began to trudge towards the bluffs.

They showed stark and black against the night sky, and by starlight they looked impossible to climb. He reached them and began to walk west along the foot, seeking a break.

He walked through the night without locating any climbable section. As the false dawn spread opalescent light over the desert, he halted, not wanting to risk further dehydration. He made a rough shelter where a jumble of stone spread over the sand, using his bedroll to fashion a tent that would afford him some small degree of protection from the sun, then waited for the dew to form. When it did he moved slowly amongst the cactus plants, going down on his knees to lick the moisture from the bulbous growths. He found a cluster of barrelhead and cursed his lack of a knife. With a blade, he might at least have cut some of the plants and pressed out the moisture they retained. As it was, he lapped dew like an animal and returned to the shelter to curl up and sleep away the day.

When dusk came again, he rose and continued west along the line of the bluffs. A thin crescent of moon afforded a little extra light so that his progress was a fraction swifter than before. Even so, he knew that he had to find water within the next twenty-four hours: without it, he would become too weak to attempt the climb.

At exactly 1.10 A.M. he found a way into the bluffs.

He had almost forgotten that roads existed in the desolation of the arid terrain. Indeed, in this section of Texas there had never been too many; but the block-house had to have an entry point somewhere, and Chance had found it.

It was covered with sand, and there was cactus growing through the cracks, but it was still a road. A service track, presumably built to allow the construction crews in. It ran arrow-straight to the north, and curved away into the bluffs to the south. He might have missed it had his physical senses not registered a slight change in the texture of the ground. Enough that he stopped and tested the surface. Then went down on his knees to scrape at the sand – and find tarmac three inches down.

Knowing the road was there, he was able to pick out its course amongst the boulders. He turned onto it, trudging doggedly up the slight incline. Either the terrain or the whim of the builders had dictated that the road avoid a straight line. Rather than cutting directly into the bluffs, it ran in a series of curves as it proceeded into the hills. Long sections were hidden beneath the overlay of sand, and others were lost where rubble had fallen from the bluffs. Several times Chance was forced to detour, climbing around barriers of piled rock or skirting fissures too wide to jump. But the gradient continued steadily upwards, becoming steeper as he moved farther into the ridge.

As the sun showed against the eastern skyline, he reached the summit. He was close to exhaustion, his hands bloody and his muscles protesting at the exertion. He leant against a flank of rock, staring around him. With the advantage of height he was able to follow the twisting contours of the road, and see why he had missed it from the helicopter. Apart from the natural detritus that now camouflaged it, it had been built to deceive the eye, the curves hidden in the shadow of the bluffs or overhung by outcrops of stone. It reached the summit and must, at some time, have descended into the bowl below. Now it ended on the summit. Ten feet from where Chance stood, it fell away on the edge of a cliff.

He went to the edge and studied the descent. The bowl was still in shadow, but he could make out the white shape of the block-house, and the sky was now light enough that he could see where explosives had been placed to destroy the road. It had originally gone down the gentler slope to swing round west of the house. Now there was just the cliff and the rubble piled below.

Chance shrugged and settled against the rock to sleep.

It was mid-morning when he woke. The sun was fire on his face and his lips were cracking. His tongue felt furred and there was a sour taste in his mouth. He forced himself to swallow dry rations, then went back to the cliff.

Survival is in the will.

And I will.

It was easier than he expected. With the sun lighting his way he found the slope relatively gentle, the rubble blown out by the explosion that had destroyed the road providing him with foot and handholds. He came off the scarp and felt grass under his feet. Four hundred yards down, he could see the fence.

He stood up and began to walk.

The grass felt good and a mood of curious optimism came over him. He held the rifle casually, studying the block-house as he drew level, wondering how the old man would react to his presence. There was no sign of him around the house and the metal-shuttered windows remained blank as Chance skirted the fence and saw the gate.

Then he saw the old man.

He was on a lean-ribbed pony, riding bareback as he herded cattle towards the stream.

Chance put the M18 on the grass at his feet and lifted his arms so the oldster could see his hands were empty. Then he shouted.

The old man turned and Chance saw the Winchester in his right hand come up to his shoulder. He dropped as a bullet whistled over his head and the old man yelled:

'Stay down or you're dead!'

'Either way,' Chance grunted. And stayed flat.

Chapter Thirteen

'Who the hell are you?'

Chance twisted his head so that he was looking up into the muzzle of the Winchester. The 30-30 bore was unnervingly large that close to his face.

'Matthew Chance.'

'Never heard o' you.' The old man stood with his feet wide apart in dusty high-heeled boots. 'What you doin' here?'

'Feeling thirsty,' Chance grunted.

'A goddam comedian!' The old man spat. It landed an inch from Chance's face. 'Any good reason I shouldn't kill you?'

'I got news from Austin. And I want to get at Garth Chambers.'

There might have been surprise on the old man's weather-beaten features. It was hard to tell under the tan and the network of lines.

'How'd you get here?' he demanded.

'Stole a Jeep from the column Chambers sent out. I ran out of gas a couple of days back. Been walking since.'

The old man chuckled. 'Yeah! I reckon you would be thirsty. If that's true.'

'Take a look at my face,' Chance grunted.

'You got a point,' the old man admitted. 'Only one thing wrong with the story.'

'What's that?' asked Chance, feeling his neck begin to ache.

'The Nightmen. They'd have jumped you.'

'They did.' Chance grinned bitterly. 'The first night out. Killed nine men. I took the Jeep after that.'

'An' then you just drove along until you run outta gas.'

'No.' Chance saw the trap. 'There was a pit over to the west I didn't want to get close to. They jumped me coming over a ridge, but I outran them. Followed a deep ravine along.'

'Yeah?' prompted the old man. 'Wanna tell me how you got across that mother?'

'Jumped it,' said Chance; evenly. 'There was a broken ridge about thirty miles east. I ran the Jeep up and over.'

'Christ!' There was a fraction of doubt in the old man's voice now. 'That's wild enough I almost believe it.'

'It's the truth,' Chance said.

'An' then you just naturally stumbled on this place?'

'No.' Chance looked down at the grass, then up again. 'I knew you were here. I was looking for you.'

'How?' rasped the oldster. 'An' why?'

'It's a long story.' Chance shook his head. 'Can I have a drink?'

'Got no truck with Chambers' people,' was the answer. 'Got no water for 'em, either.'

'I'm not with Chambers,' Chance snarled. 'I'd like to kill the bastard.'

Abruptly, the old man chuckled again.

'All right, feller. Get up on yore feet an' walk real slow down to the stream. Leave that fancy rifle where it lies an' don't try nothin'.'

Gratefully, Chance climbed to his feet and walked down to the stream. He was conscious of the Winchester pointed at his back, noting that the old man kept far enough away there was no opportunity to grab the gun.

He went down on his knees by the water and splashed his face. It felt good. Then even better as he scooped up a palmful to moisten his parched mouth. He felt his tastebuds return to life and drank sparingly, wary of bloating his belly. The old man grunted his approval.

'You know how to drink. What you say yore name was?'

'Chance,' he repeated. 'Matthew Chance. What's yours?'

'Elroy Fairweather.' It was said with a degree of pride. 'My momma was Cherokee. Now tell me how you knew I was here.'

Chance squatted on the grass. Fairweather stood six feet away with the Winchester still aimed and cocked.

'I came out of Louisiana.' Chance picked his words carefully, not yet ready to reveal his connections with Chambers. 'I got picked up on the border and offered a choice: join a chain-gang or fly a helicopter.'

'It was you!' The rifle came up to Fairweather's shoulder. 'You was the pilot brought that goddam pipsqueak lootenant an' his men.'

'I didn't have much choice.' Chance spoke fast. 'Like I said – fly or join a chain-gang.'

'All right.' Fairweather remained suspicious. 'I can swallow that. But it don't explain.'

'No,' Chance agreed, 'but give me time.'

'Got plenty o' that.'

'OK. Chambers got word of this place and the idea to use it as some kind of fort. He says he can control the border from here. He sent a column out to take it.'

'Not much chance,' grunted Fairweather. Then chuckled again. 'Eh, Chance?'

'I told him that. But he's crazy. He's power-mad. He sent the lieutenant you saw with the Jeep I stole and two APCs. Also two trucks.'

'Figgerin' to siege me out, eh?'

Chance didn't say that had been his idea. Instead:

'Something like that. I was forced to go along. Then the Nightmen jumped us and took out one truck. I got hold of the Jeep and made a run for it. The rest you know.'

'Except why you wanted to come here,' the old man rumbled.

Chance shrugged. 'Where else could I go?'

'Where was you headed in the first place?' Fairweather relaxed slightly.

'I was looking – *am* looking – for my wife,' said Chance. 'And my kids.'

'An' you figgered to find 'em in Texas? How come you don't know where they are?'

'We were divorced,' Chance answered. 'I was flying supplies in the Indian Ocean when it happened. The bombing, I mean. I came back to find them. I need to know they're safe.'

'Or dead,' said Fairweather sombrely. 'Lotta people died then. More since.'

'I still have to try,' Chance said.

'Yeah.' Fairweather nodded. Then: 'Why's it you want to kill Chambers?'

'He organized the divorce.' Chance's voice was bitter again.

'Eh?' Fairweather frowned, though it didn't show much through the seams on his face. 'How come?'

Chance stared at the Winchester, then at the old man's face. He decided to risk it.

'Chambers is Stephanie's father.' He saw the jet-black eyes narrow. The forefinger tighten on the rifle's trigger. He continued fast. 'He fixed everything. Took my wife and kids from me. I had a small airline – he threatened to break me. There wasn't a damn' thing I could do. He stole my wife. Stole my kids.'

'He's good at that,' Fairweather agreed. 'That why you come to Texas?'

'That's right.' Chance nodded, relaxing as he felt the tension decrease. 'I thought they might be here. Or Chambers would know where they are.'

'And?' Fairweather prompted.

'He offered me a deal.' Chance kept his voice even. 'Fly for him, and he'd try to locate them. He's short of pilots.'

'Ain't got much fuel, either,' grunted Fairweather. 'Ain't actually got much of anythin'.'

'He's looking to get bigger,' Chance said. 'That's why he wants this place.'

'I know it. Ole Garth's one greedy sonofabitch.' Fairweather gestured with the Winchester. 'All right, stand up. I reckon I believe you. Come on over to the house.'

Chance stood upright as Fairweather turned without further preamble and strode towards the fence. He paused at the gate, gesturing casually with the rifle.

'Best go bring that thing. What is it, anyway?'

'Armalite M18.' Chance lifted the gun by the combined sight/carrying handle. 'Made by Colt.'

Fairweather nodded thoughtfully as he swung the gate open.

'How's it perform?'

'Good,' said Chance, following the old man into the compound. '.233 calibre with an accurate range of 500 yards. Carries a thirty-round clip and it's light – only weighs just over six pounds.'

'I'll stick with this.' Fairweather patted the Winchester affectionately. 'Got a lotta fancy guns stored away, but I got kinda used to my old 30-30.'

He pushed the gate closed and turned a key in the lock, then ambled bow-legged up to the house. He produced a second key from inside his faded levis and opened the door. Chance noticed that it was a wood veneer over metal.

'Welcome to the hacienda.' Fairweather propped the Winchester in a rack beside the door. 'Dump that Armathing there.'

Chance did as he was ordered and looked around the room. Apart from the metal shutters covering the windows, it looked like a typical Texan ranch-house. The walls were rough white plaster, contrasting with the rich, red glow of the timbered floor. Navajo rugs were scattered over the planks and there was a huge stone hearth with cowhide easy chairs facing a stack of logs. The rest of the furniture was solid, dark wood: a long table with ten chairs around it, and some cabinets containing nick-nacks and ornaments. Chance saw what looked like an original Remington bronze in one cabinet, and when he looked closer at one of the paintings that broke up the white expanse of wall, he realized it was a genuine George Catlin. There was a feeling of money to the room, combined with simple taste and a rough comfort.

'This yours?' he asked.

Fairweather chuckled. 'Is now,' he said. 'I'll tell you about it over food. You hungry?'

Chance nodded.

'I'll fix us something,' said the old man. 'But you take a shower first. You smell kinda rank.'

'A shower would be good,' Chance agreed. 'Where do I go?'

Fairweather pointed at the wide stairway set into the far wall.

'Any door. They all got facilities. One at the end's mine, but you just take whichever else you fancy.'

He disappeared through a door beside the stairs as Chance began to climb. The grey-haired man looked back as he reached the balcony, working out the dimensions of the place. It seemed that the entire ground area was taken up by the room, the remainder of the building – apart from the upper level – running back into the hillside. There were doors either end of the balcony, and when he opened the nearest he saw that it gave access to the exterior balcony. He opened the next door and found himself in a luxurious suite of rooms. There was a lounge with more Indian rugs on the polished wood floor and comfortable-looking leather furniture. A well-stocked cocktail cabinet stood against one wall and windows on the other. A genuine Remington hung beside a Karl Bodmer, and when he entered the bedroom, he saw a Matisse. A door in the bedroom revealed a shower cubicle and a bath sunk into the floor. There were no windows, but modulated fluorescent lighting came on as he swung the door open. The walls were tiled, two of them depicting Texan landscapes so that the effect was one of space and airiness. He opened a cupboard and found towels stacked neatly inside, with a selection of razors and various lotions on a shelf below.

Amazed at the opulence, he stripped off his clothes and stepped into the cubicle.

The water was hot and the sandalwood soap smelled good as he scrubbed his leanly-muscled body. When he was finished he swung the shower control to *cold* and stood beneath the jet of icy water. He towelled himself dry and shaved. As he scraped the last of the stubble from his cheeks he heard Fairweather enter the lounge.

'Brought you some fresh clothes,' the old man called. 'Figger we're about the same size. 'Sides, I can't stomach the sight o' them uniforms.'

Chance grinned and climbed into the levis and denim shirt. They were brand-new, and he decided the entire block-house had to be stocked for a long, long stay. He laced his combat boots and went down the stairs to the big room.

The table was set for two with silver cutlery and bone china plates. Cut crystal goblets stood beside the crockery and a bottle of Chateau d'Yquems '37 that would have cost around $400 in the old days rested in a silver pourer.

'Nice place,' he remarked wryly as Fairweather came in with steaks, baked potatoes, and a green salad. 'You run it alone?'

Fairweather served the food, grinning.

'Hell! This place runs itself. Whole damn' set-up's automated. Got a freezer out back could feed all Austin fer a year. Got solar panels on the roof an' them windmills outside provide electricity. Got a generator built back in the hill, too. An' water gets pumped outta the stream.'

'Chambers said it's a bomb shelter.' Chance cut into his steak, watching blood run from the centre. 'Why he wants it.'

'It is.' Fairweather nodded, pouring wine. 'Belonged to my boss. Feller called Walter Coombes. He was into oil an' real estate. You ever hear of him?'

Chance shook his head.

'Ran cattle, too,' murmured Fairweather thoughtfully. 'I looked after that end. Why I'm still here, really.'

'Yeah?' prompted Chance, sipping the wine. It sat smooth and luxurious on his tongue.

'Yeah,' Fairweather nodded. 'Ole Walt was a businessman, but he never lost touch with his roots. Not like Garth. They was partners one time. But they never did see eye-to-eye. Walt figgered there was trouble comin' an' he wanted to get into shelter building. Garth didn't agree, so they split up. This place was kinda like a show-case. Walt bought the land an' built the ole hacienda quiet as he could. Why Garth didn't know exactly where it was, I guess.'

He broke off, staring moodily at his glass.

'What happened to him?' Chance asked.

'Got killed,' said Fairweather tersely. 'We rode out the bombing easy enough, but afterwards he decided to go into Austin to see how things were. He never came back.'

'Chambers?' asked Chance, seeing anger tauten the old man's features.

'Hung him,' grated Fairweather. 'I run back here. Been here since.'

'So we both got a grudge.' Chance sipped more wine.

'Goddam right!' Fairweather snapped. 'An' one day I'm gonna settle it.'

Chance nodded. Then: 'He said Steph was last heard

from in California. Claimed to have contact there. Is that possible?'

'Hell, no!' Fairweather shook his head. 'Walt kitted this place out with the best radio equipment he could buy – an' that means *the* best – but it ain't good fer nothin' except short range now. Missiles took out the satellites an' the radioactivity fouls up the signals. I get Corpus Christi once in a while an' a coupla times I raised Nevada, but otherwise there ain't nothin'. Only way to reach California is overland.'

'A plane could do it,' Chance suggested.

'Maybe.' Fairweather shrugged. 'If it had enough fuel. An' it didn't hit one o' them freak storms that blow over the mountains. No, overland's the best bet.'

He swallowed the last of his meat and stood up. Chance watched him clear the dishes and go back into the kitchen, reappearing with apple pie and ice cream. He seemed not to want to talk any more, concentrating on the incongruously homely pie as though lost in thought. When it was finished he allowed Chance to help him clear the table, carrying the dishes back into a kitchen as luxuriously appointed as the rest of the house.

'Let's go sit a spell.' He fetched two thick tumblers of the same crystal pattern as the wine goblets, and a bottle of Jack Daniels. 'Get some real pretty sunsets up here.'

Chance followed him onto the porch and they settled against the white-painted wall with the bottle between them. The sun was touching the horizon and the sky to the west was a brilliant red that faded into bands of pink before meeting the velvet blue of the encroaching night. A cow lowed down by the stream and off to the east a pony snickered softly.

'Know what I miss most?' Fairweather asked, answering himself before Chance could speak. 'The sounds. You don't hear birds no more. Ain't even no cicadas. I hear the cattle an' the horses. Guess there ain't much of anythin' else left alive.'

'No,' Chance agreed. 'I guess not.'

Fairweather filled the glasses. 'Tell me about yoreself,' he said. 'I mean, before you got to Austin.'

Chance told him and the old man nodded reflectively.

'So you got military trainin'. What rank was you?'

'Captain,' Chance replied.

Fairweather grunted and stared at the steadily decreasing band of crimson that lined the western horizon. He said nothing as the crimson went out and the night took over the sky. The moon shone an impassive silver-yellow, glistening off the surface of the stream. Stars gleamed above them, and Chance longed to hear a bird.

Finally, Fairweather said: 'What you figger to do?'

'Find Steph and the kids,' Chance murmured. 'Somehow.'

'An' Garth's yore only lead?'

Chance nodded grimly.

'Why I have to go back.'

'An' get hung?' grunted the old man. 'Ain't no way you'll ever get close to Garth now. Not after what you done.'

'Maybe there is,' Chance said quietly. 'Garth's not so powerful as he pretends.'

'Don't take but one bullet to stop a man,' said Fairweather. 'An' ole Garth's got guards all round him all the time.'

'Guards can be diverted,' said Chance. 'If you play it right.'

'How?' Fairweather sounded scornful. 'How you gonna create a diversion?'

'What do you know about the Nightmen?' Chance asked casually.

Chapter Fourteen

'The Nightmen?'

Fairweather put his glass down hard enough that whisky slopped over the brim. Chance nodded, smiling.

'Yeah, that's right. The Nightmen.'

'You're crazy,' said the old man. 'The sun fried yore brains.'

'Maybe.' Chance shrugged. 'Maybe not. I know Bergstrom and his men were scared shitless. Refused to travel by night. I know the Nightmen fought off a small army – killed eighty soldiers and took out three vehicles, according to the Lieutenant. I know Chambers has no control over them. I need to know more.'

Fairweather picked up his glass and topped it. He took a long swallow, coughed some and then craned his head round to stare at Chance.

'What the hell you got in mind?'

'I'm not sure yet,' Chance grinned. 'Like they say in the military manuals – gather information first, then plan your strategy.'

'All right.' The old man nodded doubtfully. 'What exactly d'you want to know?'

'Anything,' Chance said, more earnestly now. 'Everything. How come they don't attack you? You're close enough.'

'They tried a coupla times.' Fairweather grinned. 'An' I killed a few. After that we kinda made peace. I trade 'em beef fer information – they know most o' what's goin' on out there.'

'How many are there?' Chance asked. 'You know that?'

'Not fer sure,' answered the oldster. 'Be maybe three, four hundred livin' around the big pits. That one you came by, there's maybe three hundred an' fifty. Not countin' the kids.'

'They breed, then?' said Chance. 'They're not sterile?'

'Some are, some ain't,' was the answer. 'They prize the kids. One o' the reasons they're so mad at Chambers – they need food, medicine same as anyone. Hell! I trade 'em medical supplies, too. Chambers, though, he's given orders to shoot 'em on sight.'

'The ones I saw carried home-made weapons.' Chance clutched his whisky, the glass forgotten in his hand. 'Crossbows at best.'

'Yeah.' Fairweather nodded. 'They got a few guns, but mostly they don't need 'em. They learnt to live out in the desert an' they're real quiet. Like you found out. It's hard for them to get ammunition.'

'The crossbows were factory-made,' Chance countered.

'Sure. There was a hypermarket out on Route 35. The goddam army of the goddam so-called Republic of Texas stripped out all the guns an' ammo, but the stupid bastards left everythin' else. Guess the other bands did like my ones did – took the bows.'

'How many pits?' Chance asked.

'Six, seven that I know of.' Fairweather shrugged. 'Some big, some smaller. Maybe a thousand Nightmen in all. Maybe two thousand. I wouldn't guess there's more.'

'That's enough.' Chance's voice was eager. 'That's an army.'

Fairweather said, 'Jesus H. Christ!' Very softly.

Chance said, 'How do you contact them?'

'I don't,' the old man replied. 'They drift in round about the same time every month.'

'What time?' demanded the grey-haired man. 'How long before they come again?'

Fairweather looked up at the moon.

'Anytime now. Within a week, I'd reckon.'

'Good,' said Chance. 'You want to show me the rest of the house?'

There were two doors at the far end of the long room, one beside the stairs, the other hidden behind a hanging blanket. Fairweather dragged the blanket aside to expose what looked like a sheet of solid redwood. When he turned the handle, the door slid aside on oiled runners to reveal a passageway running back into the hill.

'Bombproof,' he grinned. 'Redwood veneer over Swedish steel. That,' he pointed to a door on the left side of the passage, 'connects with the kitchen. Bombproof door there, too.'

He led the way down the corridor, moving deeper into the natural rock formation until they came to a massive door of undecorated steel. He fumbled in his pockets for a moment, then found a bright red key that he slotted into what looked like a standard keyhole. Instead of turning it, however, he simply pushed it home and then turned a handle set into the wall. The door swung silently open.

And Chance gasped in surprise.

A cavern lay before him, floored with plastic, the craggy ceiling adorned with fluorescents that shone bright on an array of both hard and software. There were computer consoles and air purifiers; a soundproof booth over to one side contained radio equipment; a second booth held bunks; a third was fitted out with video equipment and easy chairs.

'Ain't bad, eh?' Fairweather chuckled. 'Iron Mountain wasn't the only stronghold.'

He continued the tour of inspection with the innocent pride of a man grateful for someone to talk with, someone to show it all. There was a generator room and a storage tank for the water siphoned from the spring. A dormitory held bunks that would sleep thirty bodies. There were waste disposal facilities and a massive freezer that he told Chance was entirely separate from the freezer adjoining the kitchen. There were soft drinks and hard liquor. A library that held books and video tapes and music, doubling as a lounge with seating for fifteen. There was a decontamination room and silvery protective suits hanging in a steel closet. It was a redoubt of enormous ingenuity: thirty people could have lived there in relative comfort.

Chance was impressed.

Fairweather was pleased.

'Walt sure planned it good,' he said proudly.

'Yeah.' Chance was surprised his voice failed to echo in the subterranean chamber. Then he saw the sound baffles located around the walls and ceiling. And was more impressed. 'Yeah, he sure did.'

'There's an armoury, too.' Fairweather produced a new key. 'Right here.'

Chance walked into a room that might have equipped a small army. M16s were racked along one wall, ammunition and magazines stored in lockers below. There were Browning 9mm Automatics and Magnums from both Colt and Smith & Wesson in .357 and .44 calibres. He saw four M60 machine guns with their ammo belts in containers behind; a dozen Ingrams, complete with extra clips and boxes of .45 shells. There were hunting rifles with scope sights and infra-red night sights.

He whistled softly as Fairweather's grin got wider.

'Walt believed in planning ahead,' he murmured.

'Sure did,' nodded the old man. 'He figgered things'd break down after a war an' he wanted to be ready. Didn't quite figger on it happenin' the way it did, though.'

Chance nodded. No one had. Not exactly. A fast missile war, perhaps; or a conflict limited to Europe. But the way things had gone – the economic struggles; the bush wars in

South America; the Libyan Conflict, they had all built up in a slow process of attrition that had drained America so that the final, swift eruption of the nuclear war had come as the shattering blow that reduced the United States to chaos. To North America's current situation.

'No wonder Chambers wants this place,' he murmured.

'He ain't gonna get it,' rasped Fairweather. 'No way.'

Chance turned in a slow circle, studying the weapons Walter Coombes had stored. Then he grinned at Fairweather.

'We've got the guns,' he said; eagerly. 'If we can get the men to use them we've got Chambers.'

'You're outta yore head,' grunted the old man.

But he listened as Chance began to explain.

Chapter Fifteen

Chance woke as the outer door opened. Glancing at his Rolex he saw that it was 2.37 A.M. He reached over to the control panel mounted in the bedhead and flicked on the lights, sitting up as Fairweather came into the bedroom.

'They're comin',' the old man said. 'Get ready.'

Chance was already swinging clear of the bed, grabbing for his clothes. He dressed fast, belting a Colt Magnum in .357 calibre to his waist, then hitching the heavy revolver round to his left hip where he could reach it under the combat jacket.

Ready, he went down the stairs at a run to join Fairweather on the porch. The old man pointed towards the westerly slope.

'See 'em?'

Chance followed the direction indicated and saw what looked like a shadow creeping down the incline. The moon was fatter now, shedding more light, but the approach of the Nightmen was so fluidly silent they might have reached the fence unnoticed had they not been expected.

'Leave me do the talkin',' whispered Fairweather. 'Leastways until I explained who you are.'

Chance nodded, watching the creeping shadow become individual shapes as the group drew closer.

The Nightmen halted at the gate and stood in silence as Fairweather stepped down off the porch. He was unarmed, and as he approached the gate, Chance folded his arms, putting his right hand close to the butt of the Magnum.

'Hi.' The old man's voice was casual. 'Come on in.'

He swung the gate open, but the black-clad figures remained where they stood.

'Who's that?'

Chance was oddly surprised that the voice issuing from beneath the hood was normal, accented with a Texas twang.

'Name's Matthew Chance,' Fairweather said easily. 'Friend o' mine. Enemy o' Garth Chambers.'

Something that might have been a chuckle came from the hood and the figure moved forwards. Three others followed, and Chance counted fifteen more who stayed by the gate. Some were carrying crossbows, but most appeared to be armed only with home-made weapons. He stepped forwards as they came up to the porch.

'Matt,' said Fairweather formally, 'this is Colby.'

Chance studied the man indicated. He was big, around six-four, with massive, rounded shoulders and legs that seemed to bend the wrong way. There was a crossbow slung on his back and a scimitar-like sword strapped to his waist. His eyes studied Chance through the slits in his hood. Then, with slow deliberation, he reached up and tugged the masking cloth from his head.

Chance kept his features impassive as he saw the man's face. It looked as though he had been ugly to start with, and then got worse. The left side was a mass of scar tissue, the skin a mottled purplish colour that surrounded a collapsed cheekbone dragging down the eye. That, like the right, was a milky hue with a tiny, black pupil. His mouth was lipless; lizard-like. And his hair grew in random white tufts over a wrinkled scalp that shone faintly in the moonlight. He smiled, exposing yellow teeth.

'An enemy of Chambers?' Again Chance was surprised by the normality of his voice. 'Then perhaps you're a friend of mine.'

'I hope so,' Chance said.

'He's got an idea,' Fairweather interrupted. 'Wants to put it to you.'

Colby nodded. 'After we trade. I'll listen then.'

'Sure.' Fairweather grinned with some uneasiness. 'What you want?'

Colby reached into his tunic and handed the old man a scrap of paper. Fairweather studied it for a moment, then nodded.

'All right, but you better have good news.'

'I got plenty.' Colby shrugged, one shoulder going higher than the other. 'It ain't good.'

'When is it?' Fairweather murmured. 'OK, tell yore people to cut out the cows. I'll go get the rest.'

He glanced at Chance, who remained standing on the porch, then disappeared inside the house. Moments later he returned with a plastic sack fastened at the neck with tape.

'It's all in there.' He set the sack down at Colby's feet. 'Now what you got to tell me?'

'Chambers is planning a war,' said the disfigured man. 'He wants this place as a jumping-off point. I think he's planning to invade Corpus Christi. He sent a column out – we attacked it.' He stared milkily at Chance. 'A man took off in a Jeep. He was headed this way. Some of the others got back to Austin. Our people in the city say he's organizing a full-scale army.'

'You've got people in Austin?' Chance spoke with excitement, forgetting Fairweather's instructions.

Colby went on staring at him. Nodded. Then: 'You were the man in the Jeep. You killed one of my people.'

'You ambushed me,' said Chance evenly. 'What else would I do?'

Colby grunted non-committally.

'Why did you run? You were with Chambers' men.'

'Not through choice,' replied the grey-haired man. 'Chambers didn't give me much option.'

'No.' Colby's mouth split in a lipless smile. 'He doesn't give anyone much choice.'

'Your people in the city,' Chance pressed, 'how good is their information?'

'Excellent,' Colby answered. 'Reliable. Chambers is calling his border guards in. He's using two helicopters to patrol east and north.'

'Been no choppers this way lately,' said Fairweather.

'That would alert you,' grunted the big man, his scarred face impassive. 'I think he's planning a sneak attack. He'll hope to take the ranch and use it as a forward base.'

'Like you said.' Fairweather turned to Chance. 'That bastard's ambitious.'

Chance nodded. Stared at Colby.

'You want to get at Chambers?'

Colby laughed. A dry, coughing sound.

'Garth Chambers drove us out of Austin. He destroyed our homes. He denies us medicines. Surgery. His men kill us. Yes!' His voice was harsh with rage. 'I want to get at Chambers.'

'Then you got an opportunity.' Chance's voice was fierce. 'A good one if you can get inside his defences.'

'Tell me.' Colby hunkered down in a squatting position, his knees jutting at curious angles. 'This sounds interesting.'

'It sounds long,' grunted Fairweather. 'You want a drink?'

Without bothering to wait for a reply he went inside the house to fetch whisky and glasses. Chance dropped onto the edge of the porch, facing Colby. The other Nightmen settled in a group around their leader. Fairweather passed the glasses round and filled them. Chance began to talk.

'Chambers isn't so powerful as he makes out. He's short of aviation fuel – if he's flying border patrols, then he's making some kind of gamble.'

'Corpus Christi has fuel,' grunted Colby. 'But no aircraft.'

'So it could be an all-or-nothing try,' Chance said. 'That column I was with? That was meant to siege Elroy here into handing over the shelter. My guess is that the Louisiana border's got quiet, so Garth is using the chance to take over all of South Texas.'

'How does that help us?' Colby demanded. 'With the men he's got, he'll roll right over us.'

'In a frontal assault, yes,' Chance agreed. 'But not if you play it right. How many fighting men can you muster?'

'Twelve hundred,' said the scarred man. 'Maybe thirteen. But Chambers' troops have guns.'

'You'll have guns,' Chance assured him. 'Not so many, but you won't be fighting the army.'

Colby frowned, contorting his features even more. 'How not?'

'You say you've got people in the city? Does that mean you can get through the defences?'

'In small groups.' Colby nodded. 'Not thirteen hundred. Chambers' men would spot us.'

'Not if they're going south,' grinned Chance. 'Not if they're out of the city.'

Colby began to smile again. 'Tell me more,' he said.

'How long before Chambers is ready?' Chance asked.

'Two weeks. Maybe three.'

'How long would it take you to gather your people?'

'A week. If the other leaders agree. I think they will.'

'Good.' Chance sipped whisky. 'Can your people in Austin warn you in time?'

Colby nodded.

'So we group as close to the city as possible,' said Chance. 'Let Chambers send his troops out. Give them time to get well clear, then move in. Take over while their backs are turned.'

'There'll still be guards,' Colby doubted. 'Chambers won't leave himself too vulnerable.'

'There'll be a holding force,' Chance agreed. 'But if he's really making an all-out attempt, he'll have to leave his base troops thin on the ground. Thirteen hundred of you should be enough to handle them.'

'I like it,' smiled the Nightman. 'But I'll need to ask my people.'

'That's democracy.' Chance shrugged. 'How long before you have an answer?'

Colby shrugged. 'Four days? Five at the most.'

'We'll be waiting.' Chance glanced at Fairweather. The old man raised his glass in a salute. 'I hope they agree.'

'Yeah.' Colby's smile was wolfish. 'So do I.'

The waiting was the worst part.

After the Nightmen had departed Chance asked Fairweather what he thought they would decide. The old man shrugged thoughtfully and said, 'No way of tellin'. They got their own way o' thinkin', an' it's different to ours. They ain't entirely human anymore, I reckon. Kinda like the Indians used to be, I guess. All we can do is sit it out.'

They sat it out. Chance helped the old man tend his cattle, enjoying the sensation of riding once again. They discussed the likelihood of his finding Stephanie and the children; the possibility of snatching control from Chambers. They got amiably drunk twice; listened to a lot of music. Chance even read a few books. It had been a long time since he had enjoyed so much leisure; but all the time the problem of Chambers nagged at his mind.

He was grateful when the Nightmen returned.

The moon was full by now, and he counted about fifty of them as they filed through the gate to settle in a wide semicircle facing the house.

Colby acted as their spokesman.

'There are seven pits,' he said formally, as though incanting a ritual announcement, 'and seven leaders.

Duane. Smith. Vincent. Beidecker. Leroy. Masters. Me.' The six leaders each rose as the names were recited. 'We have talked of your plan amongst ourselves and with our people. Five pits are in agreement. The other two will abide by the majority decision. But . . .'

He paused, staring at Chance. There was a silence so still it seemed the group held its breath. Chance waited for the bad news.

'You are not one of us. You are a Normal, and we have learnt that few Normals can be trusted.'

Fairweather began to protest, but Chance motioned him to be silent.

'Therefore,' continued the Nightman, 'we are agreed that you must prove yourself worthy of our aid. You must be tested as we have been tested. Do you agree?'

Chance nodded.

'You do not wish to know the nature of the test?' Colby spoke in the same formal tones.

'I want to get to Garth Chambers,' answered Chance.

'Very well.' Colby turned to face the assembled men. 'Coleman! Prepare.'

A Nightman at the rear of the group stood up and began to move through the ranks. He was no more than five and a half feet tall. He looked like a barrel on legs. He tugged off his hood and Chance saw a face that belonged on an ape. There was no hair, only wrinkled furrows that began where the skull bulged at the back and advanced in lines to where the naked brows overhung the tiny eyes. The nose was wide and flat, the nostrils flaring back in two gaping holes. The jaw was prognathous, the fleshy lower lip jutting ahead of the upper. He stripped off his black tunic to expose an absence of neck, and shoulders ridged with muscle sloping into arms like twin tree trunks. His hands were enormous. Chance noticed that he had six fingers. He stared at Chance and laughed.

'Coleman is our champion,' Colby announced. 'Fight him and win, and we will follow you.'

'And if I lose?' Chance asked mildly.

'You die,' said Colby. 'That is our way.'

Chance nodded and peeled off his shirt. He unbuckled his gunbelt and passed the Magnum to Fairweather.

The old man said, 'This is crazy! You ain't got a chance.'

'You just made a joke,' Chance murmured. 'Let's get on with it.'

The Nightmen rose to their feet and shuffled into a circle. Two axes were hacked into the grass at the centre. Both were home-made: four foot lengths of wood with heads beaten from salvaged metal, held in place with leather thongs. They were crude; and lethal.

Chance glanced up at the moon. Its light was strong enough he could see with reasonable clarity: had it not been full, Coleman would have enjoyed the immense advantage of his night vision. Chance studied his opponent. The man's huge arms were inordinately long, affording him the advantage of reach. But his legs were short: it seemed unlikely he would move with any degree of speed. His strength, judging from his physique, would easily outmatch Chance's; and with the greater length of his arms, the axe would be a deadly weapon in his hands.

Chance flexed his shoulders, poising on the balls of his feet as Coleman smiled at him from across the circle. Chance returned the smile.

'No hard feelings,' he called; with more confidence than he felt. 'Except when I hit you.'

Coleman laughed and spat on the grass.

Colby raised both arms, hands pointed at either combatant.

'Now!' And his arms dropped.

Chance hurled himself forwards, legs stretching in a dash towards the nearest axe.

Coleman dropped to a crouch and sprang forwards like some grotesque humanoid frog. The power of his legs was enough to bring his simian arm in reach of the axe.

The two men lifted their weapons together. Coleman brought his back over his shoulder, body twisting as he put his weight into the blow. Chance seized his in his right hand and lifted it from the grass in an upwards swing, the projecting nub of the head aimed at Coleman's groin.

The ape-like Nightman jumped back. Chance ducked under the blade that whistled over his head and grabbed the haft of his axe in a two-handed grip as he brought it down. Coleman grunted as the blade scored a bloody line over his forearm and swung his own back in a vicious arc.

Chance danced backwards. The Nightman was faster than he had anticipated. He clutched the axe right-handed, resting the head on his left palm. Coleman glared at him, both hands on the haft as he brought the axe over his right shoulder.

They circled, Chance moving around the shorter man.

Then Coleman made his curious frog-like jump again. His axe whistled over and down. Chance took a step back, timing his swing so that his blade struck the haft of the Nightman's weapon. His opponent's blow was deflected, Coleman's arms turned to the side so that his ribs were exposed on the right. Chance rammed his axe forwards, smashing the head against the squat man's ribcage. Coleman grunted and reversed his swing. The nub-end of his blade hit the blade of Chance's axe, and the grey-haired man felt shock run through his hands into his wrists as the weapon was knocked sideways. He pivoted, letting the momentum take him round and out of reach.

Coleman sprang forwards again.

Chance threw himself to the side, slashing back as he went. The Nightman's axe churned a divot from the grass as his blow was turned by Chance's desperate counter. He dragged the blade back and swung down again as Chance rolled clear.

Again the axe hit grass. This time it dug deep. Chance came up on his knees, lurching forwards to swing one-handed at Coleman's legs. The blade landed with a solid thud. Coleman grunted again and hopped back, his counterstroke missing Chance's head by a hairsbreadth.

Chance rolled, coming up on his feet with the axe held like a staff in both hands as Coleman performed another downwards swing. Shock sent lances of fire through his arms and shoulders as he took the blow. He felt his arms forced down by the power of it. He released the haft and brought the weapon back by his side, thrusting the butt of the haft into the Nightman's face.

Coleman's lips mashed against his teeth. Blood spurted over his jutting chin, but he seemed no more affected than he was by the cut soaking blood into his black pants.

Chance took the axe in both hands again, backing away as the Nightman waddled forwards.

He moved farther back, drawing Coleman after him. He slowed, giving the simian creature a chance to move in. Coleman closed, but he no longer used the hopping attack. Although no pain registered on his immobile features, Chance estimated the leg blow had hurt him. Slowed him, at least. He felt the presence of the watching circle at his back and moved away and round, pulling Coleman like some monolithic nemesis after him.

He reached the centre of the ring and halted.

Coleman spat blood and raised his axe above his head. Chance panted. Deliberately. He waited. Coleman speeded his waddle, the axe starting its downwards arc. Chance shifted balance at the last instant, letting Coleman's blade cut air beside him. He felt the haft rasp his shoulder as he brought his own weapon up in a reverse swing. It lacked the bone-breaking power of the Nightman's blow, but the razor-edged head struck the underside of the ape-man's left arm. Flesh parted in bloody lips and a stream of crimson jetted dark in the moonlight. Coleman's grunt was shriller this time. He tore his axe from the soil and swung wild at Chance's ribs.

The grey-haired man cat-footed back. A feral smile decorated his mouth now as he saw that Coleman was slowed, his blows weakened by the cut on his arm. He brought the axe back over his left shoulder. Coleman moved towards him, limping now, leaving bloody marks on the grass. Abruptly, Chance sprang forwards, axe arcing down and across. Coleman saw the danger and pivoted to counter the blow. The blades clashed together, sparks striking into the moonlit night. Chance felt the Nightman's strength again as his hands were jarred by the impact, but then he felt Coleman's grip loosen, the left hand weakened by the cut. He twisted his axe, hooking the curved head under Coleman's as he leant back. The Nightman gasped in surprise as his weakened hand lost its grip on the haft. His left arm swung clear. And Chance shifted balance to drive the topside of his blade into the Nightman's face.

Coleman tried to avoid the stabbing blow, but he had too little neck and his waist was too thick. The axe slammed into his face. Chance felt the cheekbone break and saw blood gout in two thick streams from the simian nostrils. The right eye puffed, more blood running from the overhung brow. Then Coleman's axe came back, swung one-handed. The shaft hit Chance in the ribs, erupting air from his lungs and pain through his side. He let the blow take him, leaning to the side to absorb the impact. He let himself fall, toppling sideways. Coleman snarled and fastened his left hand back on the haft, swinging the axe above his head.

Chance twisted as he went down, ignoring the fire lancing through his ribs as he brought his own blade round in a vicious arc.

A whimpering cry burst from the Nightman's mangled lips as the edge caught the side of his knee. His leg folded, his blow landing a foot clear of Chance's head. Chance rolled again, coming back on his feet with the axe gripped two-handed above him. He brought it down in a ferocious blow as Coleman crashed to the grass. It landed where the Nightman's neck should have been. Crimson spouted in a column from the base of the ape-man's skull. Chance felt the spine break. Coleman's mouth gaped open and blood ran thick on the grass. The tiny eyes stared blankly, then closed. Chance twisted the axe free. Coleman lay still.

Chance turned to stare at Colby.

'Do I have an army now?'

Colby stared back and nodded.

'You got an army.'

Chapter Sixteen

The Nightmen gathered.

They came from the pits like shadows in the night, a massing black-clad army in which the sexes were indistinguishable. Chance's night vision improved as Fairweather handed out the guns stored in the arsenal and he taught the mutated creatures how to use the automatic weapons. A few had military experience, and these he detailed off as squad leaders, training them in the darkness as they waited for word to come from Austin.

How the Nightmen communicated, Chance never did find out, but after a week had passed Colby informed him that Chambers' army was pulling out of Austin. The same night Chance led his guerrilla force north.

They swung wide of the enemy's line, Colby's scouts keeping them constantly informed of the Texas Army's route. They moved from pit to pit, Chance and Fairweather forced to don protective suits as they rested around the centres of radioactive pollution. The Nightmen seemed to draw strength from the pits, some weird alteration in their metabolism rendering them immune to the worst effects of the radiation. The two Normals bore the discomfort of the suits with stoic indifference, buoyed up by their desire to strike back at Chambers. The Nightmen, in turn, suffered during the daylight hours, when they were forced to seek shelter in shallow trenches that they draped with black cloth to fend off the sun.

It was a week before they reached Austin, swinging west of the city to approach along the line of Highway 290.

They encountered the first of Chambers' defences in the rubble-strewn outskirts.

Three of the Texas Militia were manning an M60, mounted to traverse the road. The scouts reported their presence and Chance and Colby held a brief council of war. Then Chance went out with two Nightmen armed with crossbows. He left them crouched in the shelter of a fallen wall as he drifted around the guards' position. He had shed his clothes in favour of a black tunic, pants and hood. He was unseen as he circled the machine gun and began to move in from behind.

Closer up, he could see the M60 was commanded by a sergeant, the gunner and beltman ordinary troopers. He fetched a length of waxed cord from his tunic, settling the toggles at either end firmly in his hands. Then, silently, he rose to his feet.

It was the signal the Nightmen had been waiting for. The two troopers lurched back as crossbow bolts drove into their chests. The sergeant gasped, reaching for the M16 propped against the rubble behind him. He never reached it, because Chance came out over the rubble with the strangling cord looping around his neck, dragging him back as the air feeding his brain was cut off. Chance drew the cord tight. The sergeant's hands scrabbled at his throat, then fell limp as his eyes bulged and his tongue jutted from between his blueing lips. Chance held the choking grip until he was certain the man was dead, then loosed the cord. Fairweather and Colby moved up as he began to strip the non-com.

'What the hell you doin'?' asked the old man.

'This is just the outer perimeter.' Chance pulled on the sergeant's uniform. 'Closer in, it'll get harder. This way, I can walk up close.'

He was right: a quarter mile deeper into the outskirts they hit a command post.

It was located in the remains of a cafe, an auxiliary

generator mounted in the back of a Jeep providing a power source for the light that spilled over the surrounding rubble. The Nightmen halted, unable to face the brilliance.

Chance had anticipated the problem. He crouched beside Colby, who was squatting with his back to the cafe, hooded face turned to the ground.

'When are those charges due to blow?'

Colby took his arm, looking at the Rolex. It was five minutes to midnight. He said, 'On the hour.'

'All right.' Chance nodded. 'I'll take the cafe. When the generator goes, you move in. And for God's sake don't kill me.'

Colby chuckled. 'I'll try not.'

'OK.' Chance snapped the safety of his M18 to the firing position. 'There'll be an officer in there. I want to take him alive.'

Colby said, 'Right,' as the grey-haired man stood up and began to walk down the road.

There was a second M60 mounted behind sandbags outside the cafe and as Chance approached the muzzle swung to cover him. He lifted the M18 above his head and shouted, 'Don't shoot! Friend!'

The two men behind the gun stared at him, then one called something and a captain stepped into the light. He was holding a Browning Hi-Power. Chance felt the short hairs on his neck prickle.

'We got trouble!' he yelled.

The captain stared at him. Then, abruptly, the lights of the city went out as the charges the Nightmen had placed around the main generators went off. Chance heard the captain say, 'Christ! What's going on?' and broke into a trot.

'Nightmen!' he yelled. 'Nightmen attacking! They killed my men!'

Confused, the officer beckoned him forwards. Chance came up alongside him and waved a salute. Past the tarpaulin draping the front of the cafe he could see five troopers grabbing for their weapons.

'What the hell's happening?' demanded the captain.

And Chance said, 'Nightmen,' as he rammed a knee into the officer's groin.

The captain groaned and began to double over. Chance slammed the stock of the M18 against the base of his neck and then snapped the rifle down to squeeze off a burst of automatic fire into the cafe.

The soldiers screamed as they died. Chance swung the M18 back in a short arc, traversing the interior as he heard one of the men behind the machine gun say, 'What the fuck?' Then grunt as Elroy Fairweather used his ancient Winchester. Chance ducked, turning to level the rifle at the generator. He held the trigger down as the second gunner went back with a red hole spouting blood from between his eyes. Sparks danced golden from the generator's casing, then became suddenly blue. There was a flash and the sharp tang of ozone. The lights in the cafe went out.

Chance fired a third burst into the building, then turned as Colby came running up, Fairweather beside him.

'Ain't lost my touch.' The old man grinned as he studied the two men he had shot.

Chance nodded, and stooped beside the unconscious officer.

'I don't have much time.'

Chance held the Magnum loose in his right hand as the captain opened his eyes and groaned.

'Go to hell!' The officer's lips curled in a snarl of defiance. 'Goddam traitor.'

'Depends how you look at it,' Chance answered; evenly. 'But I don't have time to debate it with you. How many men are left here?'

The captain glared, saying nothing.

'You got two choices,' Chance murmured. 'To die easy or hard. Answer the questions and I'll kill you fast. Refuse, and I give you to them.'

On cue, Colby took off his hood. The captain gagged.

'How many?'

The captain licked dry lips and said, 'Two hundred.'

'Where's Chambers?'

'Headquarters. The old Chambers Building.'

'Thanks.' Chance raised the Magnum and blew the man's head away. Colby looked disappointed.

'Right.' Chance ejected the spent casing and thumbed a fresh round into the pistol. 'It's all yours.'

'Except Chambers,' grated Fairweather. 'He's mine.'

'Ours,' corrected Chance. 'He's got things to tell me.'

'That first,' the old man agreed. 'But after . . .'

'Sure.' Chance nodded. 'Grab a uniform. We'll get closer that way.'

Colby was rattling off orders, despatching the Nightmen like wraiths into the darkened city. Only a few lights showed now, where independent generators or hand-held torches made tiny enclaves of light. The impromptu army faded like shadows, moving silently through the rubble, the only sign of its passage the sporadic bursts of gunfire as it encountered the disorganized opposition.

'I'll come with you.' The leader of the Nightmen snapped a clip into his M16. 'That way you'll be safe.'

'Yeah.' Chance reloaded his own rifle. 'Let's go.'

With the problem of illumination removed, the Nightmen had the advantage. They outnumbered the defenders and they could see in the dark. Chambers' holding force was confused, disoriented by the sudden absence of light and attacked savagely by a near-invisible enemy. The outer perimeters fell easily and within two hours the attackers were moving into the centre of the city.

Chambers' men fell back, attempting to group on headquarters, but the Nightmen moved faster through the shadows, cutting off groups that were annihilated while they still looked for their ambushers. More were overwhelmed by sheer weight of numbers. The Nightmen were savage in their vengeance, settling the burden of old scores with feral relish.

Chance and Fairweather let Colby take the lead as they hurried towards the Chambers Building. It was located on Guadalupe Boulevard, close to the river. There were lights still burning inside.

The three men hugged the shadows of an intersection across from the imposing edifice. There were troops on the steps leading up to the great bronzed doors with Kel-Lites in their hands and the fancy uniforms Chance recognized as belonging to Chambers' personal bodyguards. Two M60s commanded the intervening street.

'I can't go any farther,' Colby whispered. 'I can't take that much light.'

'Go take the city,' Chance said. 'We'll take Chambers.'

The Nightman nodded. Then grasped Chance's hand.

'Thanks.'

The grey-haired man smiled tightly. 'My pleasure,' he answered.

Colby faded back into the shadows with his men, leaving Chance and Fairweather alone.

'You think we can handle this?' asked the old man. 'Just the two of us?'

Chance's smile thinned.

'We're going to try like hell.'

He pointed across the street. There was a man behind each of the machine guns. Four more holding the Kel-Lites, playing the powerful beams over the darkness.

'Take the gunners. I'll look after the others.'

Fairweather nodded and moved to a better vantage point.

He brought the Winchester to his shoulder, waiting for Chance's signal.

It came in a burst of automatic fire that picked up the soldiers with the Kel-Lites and threw them back against the bronze of the doors. One of the lights went out in an explosion of glass. The others fell, beams angling crazily at the sky and the street. Fairweather's Winchester barked twice, and the machine gunners pitched back with blood running down their faces. Chance sprayed the front of the building a second time, then ran forwards.

Men showed in the doorway and he shouted incoherently, feigning panic. The bodyguards saw his uniform and held their fire. He climbed the steps with Fairweather close behind him and turned to blast shots into the empty side street.

'Nightmen!' he roared. 'They're everywhere.'

The guards began to fire blind at the shadows. Chance and Fairweather went past them into the building. There were more of the blue and yellow uniforms around the desk and the feet of the double stairway; around twenty: too many to take.

'Oh, God!' Chance let his eyes roll around the entrance hall in facsimile of confusion. 'They're killing us. They're wiping us out!'

An officer with major's insignia on his tunic slapped him hard across the face.

'Pull yourself together, man!' He sounded close to panic himself. 'Where was your position?'

'The river,' Chance mumbled. 'They killed my men, sir! We only just got away.'

'How many?' the major demanded.

'I don't know.' Chance shook his head, raising his voice so the whole room could hear him. 'You can't see them until they're on you. Like ghosts. It was horrible. They . . .'

'Shut up!' The major saw the way his men were looking. 'You'll stay here.'

'He's wounded, sir.' Chance gestured at the blood on Fairweather's tunic. 'Are there medics, sir?'

Fairweather took the cue and groaned, swaying. The major glanced at him and said, 'Up the stairs. First door. Get him up there, then get the hell back down here.'

'Yessir!' Chance saluted. 'Thank you, sir.'

He put an arm around Fairweather and hauled the old man towards the nearest stairway. Behind them, the major began to bellow orders. Fairweather winked and whispered, 'By God! We done it.'

'Not yet,' grunted Chance. 'Not all of it.'

They went up the stairs and looked back. All the attention was focused on the doors. Chance let go of Fairweather and pointed at the entrance to Chambers' office. Fairweather nodded and cocked the Winchester.

'Now!' Chance kicked the doors open. They flew back on well-oiled hinges to expose the room where Garth Chambers had first interviewed him.

Chambers wasn't there.

Instead, Major Bland was standing behind the desk, his hawkish features angry as he looked up. Chance sensed the Winchester's lifting and rammed a shoulder against Fairweather, spoiling the old man's aim. The 30-30 rifle blasted flame into the room. Bland shouted, twisting round as the slug hit his left shoulder. Blood showed on his uniform and his lean face got angrier as he reached for the .44 Ruger on his hip.

Chance went down the room fast. Even so, Bland was drawing the massive revolver before he got close. Then Fairweather's rifle barked again and the major's arm was smashed, the pistol dropping from his bloodied hand.

'Shoulda told me you wanted him alive.' Fairweather kicked the doors closed. Bolted them. 'Friend o' yours?'

'No.' Chance grinned at the plaster still covering the officer's right hand. 'Hallo, Bland. Where's Garth?'

Bland's face was pale with shock. His left sleeve was getting dark with blood. He sat down heavily in the big chair and shook his head.

'Gone.'

As he said it, his eyes flickered involuntarily towards the bookshelves. Chance followed the direction. The M18 was already pointed at Bland's chest, and when he squeezed the trigger, the four round burst sent the big chair skidding back over the polished floor. Bland's mouth snapped closed as the tight grouping of 5.56 bullets burst his heart. They tore through him, ripping out from the back of the chair so that blood and pieces of bone sprayed over the massive windows. A great fountain of dark crimson gouted from his chest, splattering over the desk to stain the streetplan he had been studying. The chair hit the window and rocked forwards. Bland's corpse tilted and he fell limp onto the floor. Blood oozed from under him, glistening on the wood.

Chance went over to the shelves and ran his left hand along the surfaces. Then he grunted and spilled books clear. Reached forwards to press the hidden button. A six by three section of shelving swung out to expose an elevator.

'He's in the room at the top.' Chance pressed a second button and the elevator whirred into life. 'Let's go up.'

'He'll have guards,' Fairweather warned.

'Yeah.' Chance went over to Bland's corpse. 'So this could be useful.'

He began to drag the body over to the elevator. Then he saw the Ingram taped beneath the desk.

'And so could this.'

He tossed the M18 to Fairweather and tore the little machine pistol loose. The magazine was loaded on a full 30 rounds. He dragged the cocking lever back and hauled the body over to the elevator. Fairweather propped his Winchester against the desk; reluctantly. Chance opened the elevator door and pushed the corpse inside.

'All right.' He beckoned Fairweather into the cage. 'Let's go see the man at the top.'

Chapter Seventeen

'You know how to use that?'

Chance gestured at the M18. Fairweather grinned and said, 'Reckon so. You set it on automatic?'

'Yeah,' Chance nodded. 'You take right: I'll take left.'

The old man grunted his assent. 'Don't forget Garth is mine.'

'After he's talked,' Chance warned.

Fairweather said, 'Sure,' as the elevator door opened and Bland's corpse fell through the gap onto a thick-pile carpet that got red in a wide patch under the body. The carpet spread wall-to-wall across a room that had windows running from floor to ceiling on two sides. There were six men in the room. Five of them were staring out the windows at the gunfire flickering in the streets below. The sixth was standing facing the elevator, his mouth opening in surprise as Bland's corpse tumbled out.

Chance said, 'The major got shot.'

The bodyguard started to ask, 'Who are you?'

Chance brought the Ingram up from his side and held the trigger down as he sprayed the room. The machine pistol spat .45 calibre slugs at a cyclic rate of 1100 rpm, the muzzle velocity 900 feet per second. The bodyguard's skull exploded in a welter of shattered bone and bloodied brain matter. Behind him, three men were hurled back against the windows, the bullets stitching red holes over their chests and bellies. Crimson ran sluggish down the glass, the sweetish odour of spilled blood mingling with the acrid burn of cordite. The sharp clatter of the Ingram was counterpointed by the heavier coughing of the M18 as

Fairweather blasted the remaining two men back against the opposite window.

There was an oak panelled door in the wall facing the elevator. It opened while the firing still echoed in the room and a man in military pants and shirtsleeves gaped out. He had a Detonics .45 in his hand that he got no opportunity to use: Chance fired the Ingram into his belly, hurling him backwards the way he had come.

Chance stepped over the corpses and dove through the open door. Fairweather flattened against the frame behind him.

Neither man fired because there was no one to fire at.

Except Garth Chambers.

The President of the new Republic of Texas was crouched in the far corner of the penthouse. His knees were drawn up tight against his chest and his arms were wrapped around his head, the liver spotted hands clutching at the balding scalp.

Chance said, 'Stand up, Garth.'

Chambers brought his arms down slowly. His small, baby-blue eyes were moist. He was trembling, fleshy lips moving soundlessly as the jowls sagging from his jaw shook. He was wearing a uniform. It was all gold braid on dark blue. There was a dark stain over the crotch of the pants.

'Matthew?' He rose slowly to his feet, leaning against the wall. 'You came back?'

'Yeah.' Chance's nostrils flared as the stink of excrement filled the room. 'With a friend.'

Fairweather looked at Chambers and spat.

'You remember me?' Then, when Chambers shook his head: 'You remember Walt Coombes? He was my friend.'

Chambers said, 'Oh, God! Please! Listen to me. We can get away. Bland's got the helicopter ready.'

'Bland's dead,' rasped Chance. 'Right now, he's holding the elevator for us.'

Chambers whimpered, tears running down his cheeks.

'It was you,' he choked. 'You brought the Nightmen here.'

'That's right.' Chance went over to the maple cabinet set against one hessian draped wall. 'They're taking over.'

'The Army,' Chambers faltered. 'The Army will come back.'

'Not in time.' Chance opened the cabinet: it held liquor. He filled two glasses with Jack Daniels. 'The Nightmen will have the city before then. You're finished, Garth.'

He set the Ingram down and handed a glass to Fairweather.

'Here's to success.'

They drank. Chambers watched them, eyes shifting wildly about the room as though he sought some means of escape. There was none: Chance stood with his back to the window opening onto the roof terrace, Fairweather blocked the door.

'Trouble with penthouses,' Chance grinned. 'You block the elevator and they're all cut off. There's no one coming, Garth. You're all alone.'

'I've got money.' Chambers lifted his pudgy hands in a despairing gesture. 'Listen! I can tell you where there's an auto. I got it hidden. It's a V8 Challenger. You can outrun anything. It's got a double tank.'

'The roads are blocked,' Chance shrugged.

'No.' Chambers shook his head eagerly. 'Only close to the cities. To the west, they're clear.'

'Where is it?' Chance sipped the whisky, enjoying the old man's fear.

Chambers told him and the grey-haired man nodded.

'Thanks. Now tell me about Steph.'

'We got a deal?' The stain on Chambers' crotch got wider. 'You'll get me out? You won't let the Nightmen take me?'

Chance grinned, looking at Fairweather. He shook his

head: 'No, Garth. I won't let the Nightmen take you. You got my word on that.'

'All right.' Chambers nodded, licking his lips. 'Can I have a drink?'

'Why not?' Chance filled a third glass and passed it to the fat man. 'It's your liquor.'

Chambers tossed half the shot down in one gulping swallow. It seemed to calm him a little, for some of the old cunning returned to his eyes.

'If you take the auto, how do I get out?'

'Maybe one of your pilots is still alive.' Chance raised the Ingram. 'Tell you what, Garth. You give me all the information you got on Steph and the kids, and I'll leave you here. Alive.'

Chambers finished his drink in a second gulp and held out his glass for more. Chance topped it again.

'She joined some crazy religious cult.' Chambers' hand shook as he clutched the glass, whisky spilling over the brim. 'The Children of the Future, it was called. A man called Bingham ran it. Aaron Bingham. That's his real name: his followers called him Father Divine. He had a place on the edge of Yosemite. Future Farm. Steph took the children there.'

'When did you last hear?' Chance asked.

'Three years ago.' Chambers emptied his glass again. 'Before we lost all contact.'

He pointed to a Gaugin.

'Behind that. There's a safe. There are letters.'

Chance lifted the painting down. Chambers recited the combination. Chance opened the steel door and withdrew a bundle of letters.

Stephanie's handwriting hit his eyes like a blow. He stared at the familiar loops, fighting the sense of loss that gripped him. The topmost letter was dated as Chambers had said. It was brief, announcing simply that Steph was taking David and Jennifer to Future Farm, where Father Divine would show them how to live. It told her father not to come after her. The part that hurt was the request that Chambers tell Chance nothing. He folded the letter and tucked it inside his shirt. Then he picked up his glass and drained it.

'He's all yours,' he said to Fairweather.

Chambers looked from one man to the other.

'We made a deal,' he shrieked. 'You gave me your word.'

'I told you I'd leave you here alive,' Chance shrugged. 'I am.'

'Not with him!' Chambers pointed at Fairweather with a trembling hand. 'He'll kill me.'

'Your problem,' Chance said, smiling. Then, to Fairweather: 'You want me to wait outside?'

The old man shook his head.

'No. You done your part. Now I'll do mine. You just leave me here. Go find that auto.'

Chance nodded and went out of the room. Chambers was weeping as he dragged Bland's corpse from the elevator and stepped inside. He closed the door and felt the cage shift under his feet. He heard Chambers begin to scream as he went down. As he reached the office below he heard a single shot.

The office was empty, still lit. Chance rummaged through the files until he found a plan of the building. He located the generator and stepped out onto the balcony. The blue-and-yellow uniforms were still below, grouped around the doors. They didn't see him as he entered the elevator that took him to the basement.

He found the generator and emptied the Ingram into the machinery. The lights went out.

The guards were screaming as he climbed the service stairs to crouch under cover as the Nightmen poured into the building. He saw Colby's big frame and shouted. The Nightman bellowed an order and Chance was surrounded by a protective ring as the others stormed through the Presidential Palace, mopping up the remaining defenders.

After a while it got quiet.

'We've got it.'

Colby came up to stare at Chance. 'The city's ours.'

'Good.' Chance began to collect spare clips. 'Enjoy it.'

'Stay,' Colby said. 'We can use you.'

'No.' Chance shook his head. 'I've got people to find.'

He waited until dawn lit the city, then walked away to find the car. He left Austin to the night.

ALSO AVAILABLE IN THIS SERIES FROM GRANADA PAPERBACKS

WASTEWORLD 1: AFTERMATH

IF CHANCE CAN'T SURVIVE
IN TOMORROW'S HELL-WORLD –
NO ONE CAN . . .

Chance is made for survival. He's seen the roughest kind of actlion there is in the 'limited' wars that ripped civilization apart and brought it crashing down like a man with his kneecaps blasted.

Now, alone in a world gone kill-crazy. Chance is coming home. To find his family in a land where blood-lust rules, where bulldozers pile corpses and the living alike into mass graves, where bloated rats fight tooth and claw with marauding bands of radiation-scarred 'zombies'. Where any human life is cheaper than a can of gasoline . . .

WASTEWORLD is a shattering new experience in action-adventure fiction. Here is the living nightmare of tomorrow, where to live is to kill – and kill again . . .

IF YOU GET IN CHANCE'S WAY –
PRAY . . .

£1.50